JODI:

The Curse of the
Broken Feather

JODI:

The Curse of the
Broken Feather

Virginia Work

MOODY PRESS
CHICAGO

© 1981 by
THE MOODY BIBLE INSTITUTE
OF CHICAGO

Library of Congress Cataloging in Publication Data

Work, Virginia, 1946-
  Jodi: the curse of the broken feather.

  Summary: When Jodi visits family friends who are missionaries
to the Chilcotin Indians, she finds her friends and their work threatened by the mysterious curse of the broken feather.

  [1. Mystery and detective stories.   2. Christian life—Fiction.
3. Tsilkotin Indians—Fiction.   4. Indians of North America—Fic-
tion]   I. Title.

PZ7.W8875Jn   [Fic]   81-11154

ISBN 0-8024-4418-O   AACR2

Printed in the United States of America

Contents

To Ken and Louise Lobdell,
faithful missionaries and close friends
with whom we labored at Puntzi Mountain.

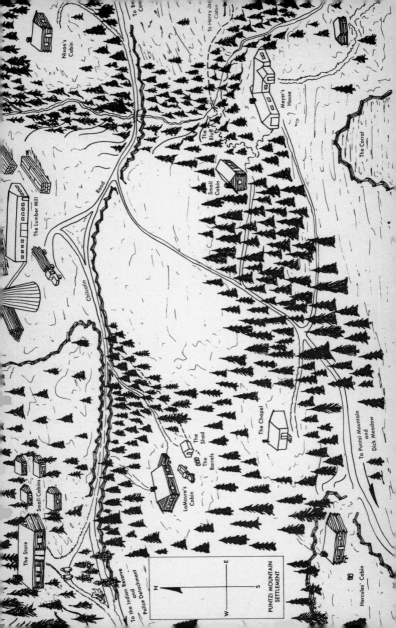

PUNTZI MOUNTAIN SETTLEMENT

Although this story has for its background a real place and a real situation, all of the names and many of the incidents have been changed. It is my desire that this book be a tribute to the many wonderful Chilcotin people whom we came to know and love during our time of service at Puntzi Mountain.

1

Puntzi Mountain

There was a freshness in the newborn day that greeted Jodi Fischer as she stepped into the back yard and strode to a log fence across the driveway. She climbed it and paused. The long, piercing rays of the sun just peering over the low mountains to the east glinted on her curly reddish brown hair, brightened the freckles that were peppered across her nose, and twinkled in her pretty blue eyes.

She smiled up at the chickadees twittering sleepily in the branches of the big pine tree towering over the barn. *Today is the day!* she thought, excitement tingling to her toes.

"First day of spring vacation," she said softly, peeling off a piece of bark. "And we're going to—" she tossed the bark into the air and leaped nimbly from the fence "—Puntzi!"

Her sudden movement and the sound of her voice startled the birds, and they rose in a cloud from the tree. She watched them fly off and then started across a field at a bouncy trot. Glancing up ahead at the big house on the knoll, she broke her stride and expertly snatched at a tall weed, pulling it clean from its stalk and sticking it in her mouth to suck up a tiny bit of sweetness.

She jogged down the driveway, cut across the dew-freshened grass to the back door, and pushed the bell.

There was a scurry of feet inside, and the door flew open.

"Jodi! I'm just about ready. Come on in!" Mary-Ann Laine, her best friend, stepped back and pulled a brush through her long, dark hair. "And take that silly weed from your mouth!" Her large brown eyes sparkled.

Jodi grinned, threw the weed outside, and stepped in. "It's good! You should try it sometime! Is there anything I can do?"

"No, thanks," MaryAnn replied, dashing back down the hall. Jodi leaned against the counter. In a few minutes MaryAnn returned with her hair combed to one side and caught in a gold barrette. She carried a big suitcase and dragged a large duffle bag.

"Here—help me, Jodi," she panted.

Jodi shook her head and took the duffle bag. "What are you bringing, MaryAnn? The whole house? We're only staying for five days, you know."

"I kept thinking of things I'd need way out there in Indian country," she replied, pushing back her hair.

Jodi glanced out the window. "Here's Dad and Brian. Let's go! We don't want to miss that bus!"

She stepped outside and hefted the duffle bag over her shoulder. Their shiny green van was not far away. Brian, her ten-year-old brother, slid open the door and looked out with gray eyes much like his father's.

"Hurry up, you two!" he called, cracking his knuckles nervously. "Do you want to miss that bus?"

Jodi screwed up her face at him. "I hope you do!" she retorted. "Don't just stand there! Pull this thing in!"

Her father glanced around. "Jodi," he said reprovingly. Then he glanced at MaryAnn and smiled. "All

10

set for a Wild West adventure, MaryAnn? Looks like you're prepared for anything!"

MaryAnn settled herself on the seat and grinned. "I've learned that when I go with Jodi, I'd *better* be prepared for anything!"

Jodi plopped down beside her as they bounced down the driveway. "I don't know what you are talking about," she said, her blue eyes twinkling. "I never get you into trouble!"

"That's a laugh!" Brian commented from the front. "At Barkerville you got us into plenty of trouble, and I bet you'll dig up some mystery out at Puntzi Mountain, too! Hey! Maybe you'll get a chance to use some self-defense that you've been learning in that class at school!"

"No way!" Jodi replied. "We're just going to ride horses and have fun!" She gazed out the window at the wooded, rolling hills and farmlands of central British Columbia. For weeks she had looked forward to this trip to the Chilcotin Indian country to visit the Meyers, their friends and fellow missionaries to the Indian people. A letter had arrived in the mail some time ago from Mrs. Meyer, inviting Jodi and Brian to come out for the week of spring vacation. Jodi had asked MaryAnn to go along, also, and now they were on their way!

She glanced out the window as they entered Richburg. It was a small town with a row of stores, a hospital, and a school. She saw an Indian man sitting on the curb, holding a bottle. Yes, the Indians were there, too. She was glad her parents were missionaries, and that there was help for the Indian people in the gospel of Jesus Christ.

11

They passed the high school.

"Aren't you glad we're not going to school?" Mary-Ann asked.

Jodi nodded.

"I'll tell you something later," MaryAnn went on, "that'll make you wish you never had to go back!"

Jodi whirled to her. "What!" she demanded. But they had arrived at the bus station, and their bus was ready to leave. Her mind churned as they checked their bags, bought their tickets, and said good-bye to her father. What was MaryAnn going to tell her?

They found seats near the front of the bus and settled into them. A little later, the bus slowly pulled out of the depot, and Jodi waved to her father for the last time. Little prickles of excitement jittered up her back and down again. A feeling of foreboding pressed upon her, but she shook it off and turned to MaryAnn.

"OK," she said. "Tell me now!"

MaryAnn sighed, her brown eyes somber. "You really don't want to hear it. I guess I shouldn't have said anything. But it's what Mona is passing around about you." She paused.

"Mona Crout!" Jodi exploded. In her mind's eye, she saw the dark-haired, heavy-set girl. "The biggest mouth in our tenth grade class," she muttered. "What did you hear?"

MaryAnn sighed again and passed her hand over her forehead. "She's saying that you're a phony—that you lead a double life. She said she saw you at a party, and she hinted that you were stoned."

Jodi turned to face the window. Her stomach tight-

12

ened into a knot, and her heart pounded in her ears. She felt her face become hot, and tears stung her eyes. She clenched her fists so tight it hurt, and the pain felt good.

"It's not fair!" she spit out. "MaryAnn, it's just not fair! Oh, that stupid—" she paused and whirled to her friend "—I know why she's doing this to me! Because Ron used to be friendly to her, and now he likes me!"

MaryAnn smiled. "Does he, really? Or is he just being friendly? I think you just *wish* he'd like you, Jodi. I don't think it helps to try to figure her reasoning. She really needs your help, Jodi. Do you think you could forgive her and be her friend?"

Jodi stared at her for a long moment. "Be her friend! That would be impossible! And I can't forget it, either. Boy, when school opens, I'm going to tell her off good!"

MaryAnn shook her head, and leaned back. Jodi stared out the window stonily. Normally she would have enjoyed this trip down the main highway through central British Columbia, but now she hardly saw the Fraser River twinkling in the sun, the forest-clad mountains, and the lakes, shimmering like jewels and reflecting God's beautiful handiwork.

Finally MaryAnn laid her hand on Jodi's arm.

"Let's not let Mona spoil our whole trip, Jodi," she said softly. "Isn't there something better to talk about? What kind of horses do you think the Meyers have?"

Jodi grinned. "I'm sorry, MaryAnn. It's kind of silly to sit and sulk, I guess. The Meyers' horses? Oh, they'll be big-footed, ploddy old things, probably. It'll still be fun with Scot to guide us around. He can make anything fun."

13

MaryAnn's brown eyes lit up with interest. "What's he like, Jodi?"

"He's neat," she replied. "Of course, I haven't seen him for years, but we used to play together when Mom and Dad worked with the Meyers at Puntzi. He's got a read bad case of acne now, his mother said in a letter to Mom, but he's a neat person. I can't really describe him. You'll just have to see for yourself."

Brian, in a seat across the aisle, grinned over at Jodi.

"Yeah, and Mrs. Meyer said he's got a girl friend now. Her name is Evangeline! How about that, Jodi. You'll have some competition!"

Jodi felt her face redden. "Oh, silly! She's just a friend, I'm sure! Really, MaryAnn! He's not like other boys. He's just Scot." She looked at Brian. "It doesn't matter, anyway. Who said I cared?"

Brian's grin widened. "I do! I saw that school picture his mom sent us on your bulletin board, Jodi."

"Oh, you!" She turned away so he would not see how embarrassed she was.

A while later, the bus entered the bustling cowboy town of William's Lake, where they would get off and meet the Meyers for the last lap of the journey. She and MaryAnn gathered up their things and looked around eagerly as the bus slowed down. Soon they would see the Meyers and be on their way to Puntzi Mountain!

The bus wheeled into the depot and stopped. Mary-Ann looked out the window anxiously.

"Do you see them, Jodi?" she asked worriedly.

Jodi shook her head. "No, I don't. But come on. Maybe they're late. I'm sure they'll be along soon." She

14

led the way off the bus. They found their bags and went to stand to one side in the busy building, studying the people that came and went.

"Boy, am I ever hungry!" Brian commented, glancing toward the cafeteria. "I hope we go get a hamburger soon!"

Jodi laid a hand on his shoulder. "Just watch, OK? And don't worry about that stomach of yours!"

"Hey! There's Mrs. Meyer!" he called out, pointing to a tall, slender woman with dark hair and glasses. She looked their way and smiled, approaching them swiftly.

"Jodi! Brian! And this must be MaryAnn," she said warmly, giving each one a hug. Dawn, a pretty girl of eleven with long, blonde braids and brown eyes, came behind her and smiled as she was introduced to MaryAnn.

"Where's Scot?" Brian asked as they picked up the suitcases and carried them outside.

Mrs. Meyer unlocked the door on their red van. "I left him home to watch things." Her voice dropped, and suddenly she looked tired. Or was it worried? She went on to explain that her husband was on an extensive trip to another area to visit the Indian people there.

Jodi helped load the van and then climbed in and sat down. What was it that she had glimpsed in Mrs. Meyer's dark eyes? She was usually so talkative, cheerful, and friendly. What was it that was troubling her now?

Mrs. Meyer glanced back at Brian as she put the van in gear.

15

"Now, how about a hamburger?" she said and turned out of the bus depot.

They ate lunch, did some shopping, and then started out over the Chilcotin road—a gravel "highway" that wound for nearly four hundred miles inland and ended at the ocean city of Bella Coola. It was a hundred miles to Puntzi Mountain, and Jodi gazed out at large ranches with hundreds of cattle and horses feeding on the new grass, at meadows linked together with a meandering river, at bunches of poplar and birch gathered along the banks of the river, and at the occasional tiny settlements with their small country stores, the Red Cross station, gas pumps, and a few homes.

"Look, MaryAnn!" Jodi pointed at a slow-paced object in the road ahead when they had traveled for a few hours. "We're in Indian country now!"

MaryAnn stared at the Indian family in a large board wagon, which was drawn by two white horses. A young boy bareback on a horse followed behind.

"Wow! You mean they still use wagons?" MaryAnn asked when they had passed.

Jodi nodded. "Sure. The Indians out here live like they did hundreds of years ago."

A little farther on they rounded a bend, and Mrs. Meyer stepped down hard on the brakes. A beat-up blue car was pointed down in the ditch. She stopped the car and jumped out. Jodi and the others tumbled from the van and stared as Mrs. Meyer slid down the bank and peered in the car window.

"Do you think someone's hurt?" MaryAnn asked, wide-eyed.

Jodi shook her head. "I don't know. Oh, there's some-one in there!" She saw a movement, and then an older Indian man slowly opened the door and crawled out of the car. Brian scrambled down the bank and helped Mrs. Meyer bring him up to the road.

"Is he hurt?" Jodi asked, running over to them.

Mrs. Meyer shook her head and pushed her glasses up on her nose. "No, I don't think so. He just fell asleep at the wheel and drove off the road. Here, help me get him in the van." They helped him into the front seat of the van, and soon they were bouncing down the road again.

The Indian man, smelling heavily of alcohol, swung his arm toward Mrs. Meyer.

"New car!" he said loudly. "I buy in town. White man, he sold me new car. Good shape, he says." He swore softly, and Jodi glanced at MaryAnn, horrified.

"White man, he cheat Indian!" the man went on, warming to his subject and flinging his arms around. "Indian, he good as white man." He turned to Mrs. Meyer and pierced her with a long, angry stare. Jodi's heart beat hard, and she clenched her fists.

"We tell white man to get out of our country. Too many of them! He take all our hunting and fishing. Big trouble coming, I tell you!" He leaned back and closed his eyes.

Jodi let out a sigh of relief. "Maybe he'll go to sleep," she whispered to MaryAnn.

"I hope so!" MaryAnn replied, gripping Jodi's arm with cold fingers. "Will he—will he get violent?"

She shook her head. "I don't think so. I wonder what

17

he meant by big trouble coming to the white man!"

"I don't know," MaryAnn replied, "but I'm beginning to wonder about this trip!"

Some time later, they slowed and turned into the rutted driveway of the Indian reserve. The old man directed them to one of the brightly painted houses that clustered around a white church. There were groups of tattered, dirty-faced children, young and old people lounging in the warm sun, and dogs everywhere.

The man got out and trudged toward his house. Mrs. Meyer swung the van around and stopped at another small house. She glanced at Jodi and MaryAnn.

"Charlie and Marie Henry live here," she explained. "Why don't you come in and meet them? Marie just came home with her baby. They're both Christians."

"Sure!" Jodi responded and slid the van door open. A few minutes later, she and the others stepped through the open doorway of the small cabin. It was starkly furnished with beds along one wall, a wood cookstove and sink on another wall, and a car seat and stumps of wood for seating. But it was clean, and Jodi smiled at the young mother who was bending over a tiny form in a basket.

There were no formal introductions, and she did not expect any. She stepped over, admired the baby, and then found a seat on a chunk of wood. MaryAnn stood uneasily by the door, and Jodi motioned for her to sit on another chunk beside her.

"That's a basket she made herself," Jodi said to her quietly. "Made of birch bark, padded with cloth, and

18

covered with buckskin. She laces the baby into it real tight, and the baby stays in that basket until it's nearly two years old. The Indian people are so clever with their hands."

MaryAnn nodded and gazed around with wide eyes. Suddenly she turned to Jodi in alarm.

"Jodi! I left my purse in the van! Do you think it's all right? Would anyone steal it?"

Jodi smiled. "I don't think so, but I'll go get it if that will make you feel better."

"It would!" MaryAnn replied firmly.

Jodi strode outside to the van. There was another house nearby, and two men sat in front with their backs to her. She reached for the door handle, and was about to slide the door open, when she heard words drifting to her from the two seated men. She stopped.

"It's the curse," one man was saying. "The curse of the broken feather!" The other man spoke too softly to hear what he said, but then the first man shook his fist.

"It's trouble for this reserve," he said. "That white man will pay for it!" The other man glanced back. Jodi opened the van door and quickly climbed inside, her heart pounding. What did they mean? What was the curse of the broken feather?

Mrs. Meyer emerged from the door of Charlie and Marie's house, followed by the others.

"Mrs. Meyer," Jodi said when they had all got into the van, "who are those two men over there?"

Mrs. Meyer glanced back to where Jodi pointed. The two men were standing now, and one was facing them.

"That's the chief, Felix Dennis," she said. **"I don't know who the other one is."** She waved to the chief, but he stared at her without expression.

"Not very friendly," Brian commented as they pulled onto the road.

Mrs. Meyer shook her head and her shoulders slumped.

"No, I'm afraid not. At one time, he was very friendly, and listened to the gospel openly. But now—" Her voice trailed off, and Jodi caught that same despairing note in her words that she had heard before. A heaviness, like a dark curtain, crept over her, filling her with dread.

The Meyers lived in a rambling, old-fashioned house that was perched on the brow of a hill. They arrived in a whirl of dust and barking dogs.

"Dawn, go get Scot," Mrs. Meyer said tiredly when they had got out and begun carrying packages into the house. "I think he's down at the corral."

Jodi glanced down that way, but could see nothing of the boy or the horses. She picked up her suitcase and sleeping bag and turned to the house. Inside, she set her things down and glanced around.

The kitchen was in spotless order, the white counter top shining and the stainless steel sink gleaming with cleanliness. The kitchen smelled fresh. There was a big window that looked over the brow of the hill and let in warm, bright sunshine. From the kitchen, she could see into the neat living room—a braided rug on the floor, a couch draped with a colorful quilt, a large chair covered with an afghan, and an old-fashioned upright piano. It was a warm, friendly house, and inside, she relaxed a little. MaryAnn had come in. Jodi turned to say something to her when she heard Scot's voice outside.

She went to look out the small window above the sink. Yes, there he was. Her heart began pounding heavily in her ribs. He was tall and slim, with a cowboy hat settled on his head. He was laughing, teasing Dawn, and gathering packages. Then he turned and Jodi ducked back from the window.

She brushed her fingers through her hair nervously as she heard his steps and laughter nearing. She must look a sight! She reached for her purse, but too soon he came into the kitchen and stood beside the table, his arms full.

She looked up at him, her heart thudding in her ears. His eyes were strikingly blue and clear. She noticed the acne blemishes on his handsome face, but it did not matter.

He put down the groceries, swept off his hat to reveal his curly brown hair, and smiled at her, his eyes dancing.

"Jodi! Welcome to Puntzi," he said gallantly, half bowing. "You're the best thing that's happened to me!" He glanced at her and smiled. "Today, anyway."

She grinned, suddenly tongue-tied, and embarrassed. She felt her face getting hot, and she hated it.

"Hi, Scot," she said lamely, wishing she could think of clever things to say to boys. She glanced at MaryAnn. "Oh, uh, this is MaryAnn, my friend. MaryAnn, this is Scot."

"Hi, MaryAnn," Scot said to her. "Jodi never told me she had such a pretty friend!" MaryAnn's face reddened, but she smiled at him as if he were the Prince of Wales.

21

He led the way to the living room where he perched on the arm of the chair, picked up a guitar, and strummed a chord.

Suddenly Jodi became aware of an Indian girl who had slipped in behind them and was standing quietly beside Scot. He glanced up at her.

"This is my friend Evangeline," he said to the strumming of his guitar. The way he said her name made it sound musical and lovely. "Jodi and MaryAnn," he said for her benefit. She smiled at them shyly, and Jodi drew in her breath sharply in surprise and amazement.

Evangeline was the loveliest girl she had ever seen! Her large, dark eyes reminded Jodi of a fawn's—soft, innocent, and dewey fresh. Her hair was cut short and curled back gently from her face, and her smooth brown skin glowed with cleanliness and health. She wore an attractive cowboy shirt, jeans, and expensively decorated cowboy boots.

"Do you have a horse?" Jodi asked, trying hard to think of something to say.

Evangeline smiled again, revealing white teeth, and glanced at Scot before she answered.

"Yes," she said, her voice low and musical. "Come on, I'll show you." Scot strummed one last chord and stood up. Jodi snapped out of her daze and followed Evangeline out of the house. Suddenly she slowed and glanced at Scot.

"Who is she, Scot?" she asked, her eyes still on the girl's slender form ahead. "She's not Chilcotin, is she?"

"Evangeline Leech," he replied, looping his thumbs

through his belt holes. "She's from up north. Some kid, huh!"

Jodi nodded, feeling a surge of jealousy and fighting it. "Is she visiting?"

"No, she's staying with her stepfather. He's—well, I'll tell you some other time. Come on." Evangeline had climbed the log fence corral and glanced back at them. Scot ran ahead and climbed up beside her.

Jodi scrambled to the top, too, and behind her came MaryAnn, Dawn, and Brian. They sat on the top log and studied the horses below. Jodi's eyes jumped quickly over the large-footed ponies that belonged to the Meyers and rested on a handsome dark Morgan standing by himself.

Evangeline called something to him softly, and the horse raised his head and nickered. He walked over to the girl and explored her hands with his soft lips. She brought out a lump of sugar from her pocket. Then she eased off the fence and sat on his back.

"His name is Thunder, and I can ride him anywhere like this," she told Jodi proudly. "He understands me. Watch." She leaned forward and said something in his ear, and the horse began trotting around the corral. Another signal, and he started loping, then a sharp tug on his mane and he stopped. Jodi smiled.

"Wow! That's pretty good! Did you train him yourself?" she asked, reaching over to rub around his ears.

Evangeline slid from the horse's back to the ground in one smooth motion. "He was my father's horse," she said softly, her face hidden in his mane. She reached up on the fence for the bridle.

23

"I should go, Scot," she said. "I've got to get home and start dinner. Bert doesn't know where I am." She slipped the bridle over her horse's ears. Scot leaped from the fence to help her mount.

She glanced at Jodi, her brown eyes flashing fiercely. "I'm proud I'm Indian," she said curtly, kicking Thunder through the gate that Scot held for her. She laid her hand momentarily on his shoulder as she passed, and then the horse was clattering up the hill. Scot closed the gate.

"What a kid," he said, chuckling softly and leaning against the log fence. "When she's on that horse, she thinks she's an Indian princess out to conquer the world." He sighed.

"Scot!" Mrs. Meyer's voice drifted down to them from the house. "Dawn! Supper!"

Jodi followed them up the hill, her stomach growling at the thought of food. On the kitchen table was a platter of what turned out to be delicious moose roast, a big bowl of mashed potatoes, steaming carrots, and fresh bread. A spice cake, just fresh from the oven, blended its smells with the others in the kitchen. Jodi went to the bathroom to wash. Like every other room, it was spotless—except for the pink towel by the sink where someone had left dirty fingerprints.

Brian, she thought, shaking her head. She turned the smudged side of the towel to the wall and stepped back into the kitchen.

"I've put your things in Scot's room, Jodi," Mrs. Meyer said after they had prayed and begun eating. "He

24

and Brian can sleep in the living room." She rubbed her forehead tiredly.

Suddenly Jodi felt guilty, remembering the suitcase she had left carelessly in the middle of the kitchen floor. And her mother had said for her to be sure to help Mrs. Meyer with the meals! This visit was definitely getting off to a bad start!

MaryAnn was full of questions about the Indian work. "Do you have a church?" she asked Mrs. Meyer.

Mrs. Meyer smiled faintly. "Well, we have a building we call the chapel," she replied, passing the potatoes to Scot. "It's really just a small cabin. At one time, it was nearly full of people who came to the services we hold. But now——" her voice trailed off as she got up to cut the cake.

"Now," Scot continued forcefully, "there's hardly anyone who comes! Not even some of them who have put their trust in Christ. Someone is turning the Indian people against us! And it's at a bad time, because——"

"Scot, don't go into that now," Mrs. Meyer interrupted. She came back to the table, and Jodi thought she saw tears glistening in her eyes. She served the cake.

"Surely there's something more cheerful we can discuss," she said, smiling with an effort.

Jodi glanced at Scot. What was it he was going to say? Why was it a bad time for them? Why did he think someone was deliberately turning the Indian people against them? He winked at her over his cake, as if to say he would tell her later. But she squirmed in her chair. If there was one thing she hated, it was something she could not figure out. Her father often said her curiosity and wild imagination got her into a lot of trouble. *And out of it, too,* she told herself firmly.

After dinner, she, MaryAnn, and Dawn hustled Mrs. Meyer from the kitchen and pitched into the dishes. Even Scot helped dry while Brian read a comic he had found.

"You gotta keep in good with the cooks," Scot told him, snapping the towel in Dawn's direction.

"If you're going to do that," Dawn told him icily, "you can leave the kitchen!"

Scot swooped in an elaborate bow to her. "Yes, Your Majesty!" He grinned at Jodi. "I hear you're pretty good at mysteries."

Jodi nodded, smiling. "Well, I have worked on a few. MaryAnn and I." She laid a dish down on the counter. "Got any around here we can work on?"

"Mom doesn't believe me." Scot lowered his voice dramatically and his eyes snapped. "But there's something going on! Just wait till you hear the whole story, Jodi!"

Jodi regarded him carefully. "When are you going to tell me?"

Scot leaned over to Dawn, his manner mysterious and secretive.

"Bring Jodi to the cabin," he hissed, glancing over his shoulder, "when you're done. We'll have a *clandestine* meeting." He hung up his towel and collared Brian. "Come on, Brian. Let's get set up for our clandestine meeting."

26

The door opened. "A candle *what?*" Jodi heard Brian screech. The door shut. She grinned at Dawn.

"He's a nut," she commented as they finished up the dishes. "Just how much of that was real, and how much of it was acting?"

Dawn giggled, drying her hands on a towel. "*Most* of it was acting. Well, come on, let's go over to the cabin." She reached for her jacket.

"Is it very far?" MaryAnn asked, peering out the big window into the darkness.

Jodi grabbed her jacket and dashed out the door, MaryAnn close behind.

"Don't you have a flashlight?" she asked, grabbing Jodi's arm.

Dawn turned down the trail through the woods. "I don't need one," she said. "I could go through these woods blindfolded. Anyway, there's some starlight."

Jodi glanced up. Stars were glimmering in the dark, velvet sky. "Starlight is cold," she commented, shivering.

The trail came out of a stand of trees and went along the brow of the hill. Dawn paused, and Jodi and Mary-Ann huddled close to her. Far away, a coyote yapped, and closer, another one answered. Down in a clearing below them lights from a group of small Indian cabins shone out like eyes in the darkness. Dawn clutched Jodi's arm.

"Someone's coming!" she hissed.

Jodi glanced back in the woods, goosebumps crawling on her arms.

"Let's hide!" she said, pulling the other two girls with her behind a fringe of bushes nearby. She strained her eyes in the dim light. She could hear the rustling of the bushes, and then she heard soft footfalls.

A dim shape materialized from out of the woods following the same path they had been on. It was a man, stooped over. He wore a hat of some kind, and as he got nearer, Jodi could see he was carrying something. Was it a flashlight?

He paused very near them, gazing over the brow of the hill as they had done a few minutes ago. Jodi held her breath, and her heart thudded loudly in her ears. Finally the man walked on down the hill.

Jodi let out her breath. "Who was that, Dawn?"

Dawn's face loomed near hers. "Hercules," she said.

"Hercules!" Jodi replied. "Who is that?"

MaryAnn squeezed Jodi's arm. "Oh, Jodi! Let's get out of here! I'm not staying one second longer!"

"OK, come on," Dawn replied, turning back into the woods. "I'll explain everything when we get to the cabin."

2

A Horse Named Red

There was a candle flickering in the window of a small cabin not too far away.

"We call this the guest cottage," Dawn said as they came onto a small porch. "It belongs to the mission, but no one lives here now." She turned the doorknob and leaned against the door, but it would not budge.

"Scot!" she said, pounding on the door. "Let us in!"

The door opened a tiny crack. "Who's there? What's the password?"

"Oh, Scot!" his sister said, exasperated. She pushed the door open and led the way into a small room furnished with only one chair and a rickety double bed against one wall.

Scot shook his head. "For detectives, you girls sure don't know how to come to a clandestine meeting!"

"Yeah, we've got the candle, too!" Brian commented, stretching out on the bed.

Jodi grinned at him and sat down beside him, the springs squeaking beneath her. Scot pulled up the chair, and the others plopped down on the bed.

She took a deep breath. "OK, now," she said to Scot, "tell me who that Hercules guy is, who Evangeline Leech is, and about her stepfather, what trouble you guys are in, and what's the curse of the broken feather."

29

"Hercules!" Scot said, looking quickly at his sister. "When did you see him?"

Dawn motioned toward the path. "On the way over here. On the trail. He's a real funny old man, Jodi, who's lived here for a long time. He's a trapper and a guide. He's white, but he doesn't like a lot of white people in the area."

"He says they take away from his trapping and hunting," Scot finished for her. He changed his voice to sound creaky like an old man's voice. "Pretty soon all the game'll be gone, and what'll old folks like me do? I gotta live, too!"

Jodi laughed at Scot's imitation. "Sounds like he's a character. Now tell me about Evangeline Leech."

"Scot's good at that!" Dawn put in, and then ducked behind MaryAnn, laughing, when he lunged toward her.

He settled into his chair once more and turned to Jodi. His eyes were serious now, and his voice was low.

"Really, Jodi, it's a sad case," he began, gazing at the flickering candle. "She has such a lot of potential. She's from up north, like I said before, and her real father was killed several years ago. It nearly killed her, too, because she practically worshiped her father. Then her mother married this Bert Leech. I can't imagine why! He's a lazy—" he paused, searching for words.

"Slob," Dawn said.

Scot nodded. "Yeah. He's white, and he lives off the Indian people by setting himself up as their band secretary, whatever that is. He's got a terrible drinking problem, and I wouldn't trust him farther than I could throw my horse with my little finger." He sighed and shook his head.

"Anyway, they moved down here, and a few months ago, her mother ran away with another man, leaving Evangeline with this Bert Leech. She hates him, and she's afraid of him, but he's all she's got. She comes and stays with us when he's really drunk." His voice faded away, and Jodi blinked at the tears that stung her eyes.

"OK," she said huskily. "Now tell me about the trouble you're in."

"I know the answer to that one," Brian answered suddenly. Jodi looked at him as if she had just seen him.

"You do?" she asked.

He nodded and brushed his blond hair from his eyes. "You would, too, Jodi, if you would just think. It was in the letter Mrs. Meyer sent to Mom. Something about the mission moving the Meyers out if things didn't open up here." He shot an inquiring glance at Scot.

Scott nodded. "You're right, Brian. See, we've been here for sixteen years—all my life, Jodi. And at first there were quite a few who received Christ and began living differently. But very few could really stand for the Lord when the pressure was on. And, recently, even the old faithfuls have turned against us." He paused, running his fingers through his curly brown hair.

"The mission has given us until the end of the month," Dawn added. "And if things aren't better by then, we'll have to move."

Scot leaned forward suddenly.

"But I know someone is trying to get us to leave!

31

We've heard things from the Indians who are friendly to us. There have been accidents, fences torn down, rumors flying around." He stood up suddenly and paced to the candle. After staring at it a few moments, he turned back to Jodi. His mood changed.

"Well, that's your mystery," he said, smiling. "We better go back. Mom'll be worrying."

"Hey!" Jodi said, hopping up from the bed, and glancing around. "Let's us girls stay in here tonight! Maybe we could find out something about the mystery!"

MaryAnn rose from the bed, shaking her head. "No way! I'm going back to the house, and I'm going to bed. I'm dead tired!"

Scot laughed. "You girls couldn't stay in here! You'd be afraid of the boogey man all night. And of all those bears that come creeping out of the woods and *grab* you!" He clutched Jodi's arm. She jumped and screamed. The two boys roared with laughter.

"OK, smarties," Jodi said indignantly, stepping out into the dark. "Leave that candle, because we're coming back, and we're staying the night!"

Somehow Jodi accomplished the impossible. Even now that they were settled in the small cabin, and she could hear MaryAnn's breathing beside her, she did not know how she had talked her into coming. She stared into the darkness, thinking about Evangeline. Her stomach tightened into a hard knot as she thought of that pretty girl living with someone like Bert Leech.

No wonder Scot was nice to her! she thought. She remembered the urgency in his voice as he said that someone was trying to force them to leave. Who would it be? And they never did talk about the curse of the broken feather! What did it all mean? She rolled over and sighed.

What was that? Footsteps! They were coming closer. She held her breath, her heart pounding. Was it Scot, coming to tell them something? The steps circled the cabin. Whoever it was, they were not trying to be quiet!

Jodi sprang from her sleeping bag, groping on the floor for the flashlight in the dim light from the quarter moon.

"What—what is it?" MaryAnn raised up on one elbow, her hair falling over her shoulders like a cascade of dark water.

Jodi glanced at her. "Listen! Footsteps, MaryAnn! And they keep going around the cabin. I'm going to try to see who it is!" She ignored the low moan from MaryAnn and tiptoed over the cold floor, gripping the flashlight hard.

Now the steps were by the bathroom. She crept into the tiny room and peered out into the dark. It took several seconds for her eyes to adjust to the dim light, but then she saw a movement. Or was it her imagination? Had she really seen a dark shape disappearing around the corner of the house? Suddenly a scream pierced the night!

Jodi jumped and let out a strangled scream herself. Then she remembered MaryAnn and dashed back into the other room.

Dawn's white face appeared in the beam from Jodi's light, but she could not see MaryAnn.

"Jodi!" Dawn was saying sleepily. "What's going on?"

Jodi prodded MaryAnn's sleeping bag. "MaryAnn! Why did you scream? Come out of there!"

MaryAnn's white face emerged from the sleeping bag. "Oh, Jodi! I couldn't help it! Those—those steps came around here, and then someone shone a light in that window!"

Jodi glanced at the window, padded over to it, and gazed out into the darkness. *Nothing!* The footsteps were gone, too. She climbed back into bed.

"Well, MaryAnn, I think your scream did the trick. Whoever that was, they sure took off!" She smiled at the thought.

Dawn laid back down. "I wonder who that was!"

"I bet it was the boys!" Jodi said suddenly. "They would like to see us scared, and go back to the house. Boy, wait till I get my hands on Brian!"

She rolled over and closed her eyes. Someone was chasing her, but she could not move her legs! It was Evangeline on her dark horse, laughing like a witch. Scot was somewhere, laughing, too. She gave a mighty leap and then was falling. Landing with a heavy bump, she opened her eyes.

The sun was streaming cheerily in the window, and above her, on the bed, MaryAnn was giggling. She had rolled out of bed. She staggered to her feet and pulled her sleeping bag up on the bed.

"Nightmare?" MaryAnn asked.

Jodi groaned. "I'll say!" Just then there was pounding on the door.

34

"Come on, you sleeping beauties!" Scot was yelling. "Up and at 'em! Breakfast is being served, but if you aren't there, I'll eat your share!" With that he was gone.

Jodi rubbed her eyes, stretched, and pulled on her clothes. Outside, the air was crisp and clear, smelling of pine and fir. The sun beamed brightly through the branches of the trees, and a chipmunk scolded them as they followed the trail back to the house.

Mrs. Meyer's dark head was bent over her Bible as she sat by the big window. When Jodi stepped into the the kitchen she looked up and smiled.

"Looks like you girls were tussling with tigers last night!" she said. "Go wash up, and then you can make toast. The porridge is hot on the stove."

Jodi hurried through the kitchen, hoping that Scot would not see her, washed her face, and brushed her hair. Brian and Scot sat at the far end of the table with piles of fishing lures, fishing rods, and all kinds of tackle lying around them. They were deep in their talk of their favorite sport.

Jodi served up the porridge, and the girls sat down to eat.

"Did you have a good sleep?" Mrs. Meyer asked, pouring herself another cup of coffee.

Jodi cleared her throat. "Well, once we got to sleep we did, but we had a little problem." She glanced down at Scot and Brian. "I think the boys know more about it than we do!"

Both boys looked up, astonished.

"Know more about what?" Brian asked sharply.

"About someone coming and tromping around the

cabin last night," Jodi retorted, her voice rising. "And shining a light in the window to scare us!"

Mrs. Meyer raised her eyebrows at Scot. "Well?"

He looked up, bewilderment in his blue eyes. "Is this some kind of a joke? I was dead to the world last night. I don't think I moved a muscle all night."

"Me, too," Brian put in. "You must have had a nightmare, Jodi."

She shook her head. "No, it was before I got to sleep!" She glanced at MaryAnn and Dawn. "I guess that leaves us with another mystery. We'll have to have another one of Scot's candle meetings." She looked at him, and he grinned back at her, his eyes twinkling.

She and MaryAnn helped Dawn clean the kitchen until it sparkled, and then they helped her with her chores. Jodi paused while sweeping the kitchen floor and glanced out the window. What a beautiful spring morning! All the fear and dread from last night was gone, and she felt ready to tackle anything.

"Those rugs could stand shaking, too, Dawn," Mrs. Meyer said, jolting Jodi out of her thoughts. She finished sweeping and then grabbed several throw rugs.

Outside, she glanced toward the corral. Is that where Scot would be? She shook her head impatiently and turned to shake the rugs. If only she could get started on this mystery!

"Here, I'll finish up," Dawn said, taking the rugs she held. "You go on down to the corral. I know you want to talk to Scot." She smiled, and then began shaking a rug.

"Thanks, Dawn," Jodi replied, heading for the trail to the corral. Suddenly she was startled by the thudding of hooves behind her, approaching quickly. She glanced back. Evangeline! She stepped off the trail and glanced up at the pretty girl as she rode by.

"Hi," Jodi said. But either the girl did not hear or else she did not want to be friendly, because she rode on by, a frown creasing her forehead and her jaws set tightly.

Evangeline clattered down the hill and pulled her horse up sharply at the corral. Scot came out of the small shed and smiled at her. But she swung down from the horse and her first words erased his smile. He strode over to her side and gripped her arm.

Jodi approached slowly, feeling jealous and uneasy. How was it that Evangeline could always captivate Scot's attention? But something was wrong, she could tell that. Would the Indian girl want her around? She had her answer sooner than she thought.

Evangeline whirled to face her fiercely. "Get out!" she snapped, pointing back to the house. "Can't I even talk to Scot?" Jodi stepped back, surprised, and felt her cheeks redden.

Scot frowned and laid his hand on Evangeline's arm. "Take it easy, old girl," he said soothingly. "It isn't her fault, you know." He turned to Jodi. "I'm sorry, Jodi. Evangeline isn't herself."

"Don't apologize for me!" Evangeline exploded, furious now with Scot. "I am too myself! I just don't like snoopers! I don't like people who stick their noses into other people's business!" Suddenly she began crying. She covered her face with her hands and turned from them.

Scot leaned over and talked to her gently. "Listen, Evangeline, it's not Jodi's fault! She may even be able to help us! Do you want me to tell her?"

The girl dried her eyes and shook her head despairingly. "I don't care," she said, her voice low. "Nothing matters anymore."

Scot turned to Jodi, his eyes reflecting how deeply he felt for Evangeline. "Last night her stepfather, Bert Leech, disappeared. She's afraid he may have been kidnapped—or worse. There's an evil force on the reserve, and it's against all white men. She's afraid to stay alone in the house, too."

"Are—are you sure he's disappeared?" Jodi asked, her blue eyes wide and her heart thumping. "Couldn't he have just gone somewhere with someone?"

Evangeline handed her a crumpled note. Jodi read it out loud.

"I won't be back. They're after me." She looked at Evangeline. "It sounds like he was running away from someone."

She shook her head. "I think he was trying to run away, but he didn't make it. His suitcase was on the bed, half-packed. And there were signs of a fight in the house. I think they got him."

"Who?" Jodi directed the question to Scot.

Scot shrugged his shoulders. "I don't know. Some of the Indian men, I guess. I don't know, Jodi. Hey, why don't we ride over there, and investigate?"

Evangeline shook her head, her large, brown eyes pleading. "No, Scot, please! That would only make things worse for me. Don't come around the reserve, and don't act like you know me if you see me. I—I guess I'll go back and see if I can move in with someone."

"How about Charlie and Marie?" Jodi suggested.

Scot smiled suddenly. "Hey, that's a great idea, Evangeline! They really like you, and they'll help you, I'm sure!"

She mounted and turned her horse up the trail. "OK," she called back. "And thanks."

Jodi sighed and leaned against the fence, her mind whirling.

"We just have to help that girl!" Scot said. "And maybe we can do that by finding out who was prowling around your cabin last night."

Jodi grinned. "You're always about three steps ahead of me, Scot," she said. "But I guess you're right. Let's go look around the cabin and see if there are any clues."

Brian joined them near the house. At the cabin, Jodi paused, glancing around. "Let's look on the ground. Maybe he dropped something." She went one way around the cabin, and Scot went the other. Brian began searching along the trail in the woods.

On the far side of the cabin, Jodi found the stub of a cigarette. She showed it to Scot.

"Hmmmm," he said, turning it over in his hand. "It's fresh and it's a Camel. So now we're looking for someone who smokes Camels."

"And someone with a flashlight," she replied. "Hey!

39

That old man! He was on the trail last night, and he had a flashlight!"

Scot nodded. "Suspect number one," he said. "Now, let's—"

Brian shouted from the woods nearby and came running up to them, holding out something in his hand.

"Look!" he said, out of breath. "I found this on the trail. There's something on it, but I can't make it out!"

Scot took the note from him and moved into the sunshine. Jodi peered at the note.

"It says, 'Scare them—out— If that doesn't—work—'" she read, and then looked up. "That's all."

She swallowed, goose bumps popping out on her arms. "Then it's true!" she said, her eyes wide. "Someone did that deliberately to scare us! We should take this to your mom, Scot."

He nodded. "I guess you're right. But I'd rather not. She already feels so terrible about everything that's happening."

MaryAnn and Dawn were playing the piano when they came in.

"Where's Mom?" Scot asked Dawn.

Dawn glanced up. "In her bedroom. She has a bad cold. What's the matter?"

Scot hesitated, looking at the note again. "We found this by the cabin. Whoever tromped around last night dropped it. I was going to show it to Mom, but now—"

"Oh, wow!" MaryAnn said softly as she read the note over Dawn's shoulder. "Let's move back to the house, Jodi. I'm not staying there one more night!"

Jodi nodded. "OK. But I don't think we should

40

bother your mom, Scot. Let's just move back, and that'll settle things down."

Scot nodded. "I'll put this in my room."

When he came back, Jodi paced nervously to the window.

"I'd sure like to get out and go riding," she said.

"Come on, then," Scot said. "I'll go with you. Anyone else want to come along?"

Dawn shook her head. "I promised Mom I'd make some bread. We're almost out."

"Bread!" MaryAnn exclaimed. "You know how to make bread? Would you show me how?" Dawn nodded, and they went to the kitchen. Jodi, Scot, and Brian went down to the corral.

"Which one do I get?" Jodi asked, surveying the three horses. "Oh, that one over there is kind of nice, Scot. Can I ride him?" She pointed to a slender, long-legged bay.

Scot shook his head. "I've been trying to break that one," he said. "He's still a little wild. Why don't you take old Buckskin? He's not very fast, but at least he won't give you a spill."

"You talk as if I'm a baby," Jodi replied, her pride wounded. "I broke my horse, Honey, you know. I can ride anything you give me!"

He grinned. "OK. Don't say I didn't warn you!" He bridled the horse and led him over to her. "We haven't really named him yet, but I've been calling him Red," he said, handing her the reins. "You can saddle him. Just watch him on the road—he spooks easy. I guess that leaves you with Buckskin, Brian."

Jodi rubbed the horse's nose softly. "Red! That's not a very good name. I'll think up something better for you."

Carefully, so as not to frighten him, she saddled Red and mounted. The horse threw his head and pranced around some, but she held the reins tight.

Scot mounted a horse he called Paint and led the way up the hill.

"Let's go down by the store," Scot said to her when they reached the main road. "I want to show you something."

"What?" Jodi asked.

Scot grinned over at her. "Curious, huh! Well, you'll just have to wait."

A car rattling by nearly sent Red into a panic, but Jodi's voice and the firm hold she kept on the reins held him in check.

Scot nodded approvingly. "You're doing real well," he said.

"For a girl," Brian commented mischievously.

Jodi made a face at him and glanced at Scot. She'd show this Chilcotin cowboy some good riding! She relaxed on the reins a tiny bit and laid her hand on Red's withers.

Just then a flurry of dogs flew at them from a small group of cabins at the side of the road. Red reared, pawing the air, and Jodi, caught off balance, grabbed for the saddle horn.

Scot kicked Paint closer and caught Red's bridle as he came down. For several seconds they fought to control the horse. Finally the dogs returned to the cabins, and Red settled down.

Jodi glanced over at the cabins. Trucks were parked around them and a white man was leaning against one, talking to an Indian man. Scott nodded to them, but they only stared back.

"If we wanted some clues," Scot said softly when they had gone on down the road, "this would be a good place to start."

"Who was that?" Brian asked, kicking Buckskin to catch up with Paint and Red.

"Why would it be a good place to look for clues?" Jodi asked. She glanced over at him, but he was thinking about something, and it took a long time for him to answer.

"Well?" she said impatiently.

He pulled his hat down on his forehead. "Well, first of all, that thin, dark man was Rex LaMoure, the foreman at the mill, and the other man was Henry Jack, the most powerful witch doctor in the area."

Brian whistled, and Jodi shivered.

"I don't know what those two are cooking up. Nothing good, you can be sure! We've had some trouble with LaMoure. The mill used to own our house and had water and electricity running to it. But he wanted to charge us such an outrageous price for those services when he first came to this job a year ago, that Dad decided to dig our own well and use an old light plant that belongs to the mission."

They passed a large, busy lumber mill with its huge,

cone-shaped burner belching out smoke, logging trucks parked around, and stacks of logs and lumber. She could hear the whine of saws, and could smell the tangey scent of pine.

"Anyway," Scot continued, "LaMoure didn't like it, and he came over when Dad was digging the well and threatened to bury him in it! Of course, he didn't do it, but ever since he's had a grudge against us."

They arrived at the small country store, dismounted, and went in. Inside, there was a little of everything necessary for life. Jodi wandered around, looking at the bridles, boots, saddles, and lanterns, feeling she had suddenly stepped back a hundred years in time. They each bought a can of pop and a candy bar, and went outside.

"You can learn an awful lot by hanging around here," Scot said as a truck pulled up and several Indian men got out. They finished their pop and candy, and then mounted the horses.

"He's settled down pretty good," Jodi said as a big logging truck roared past. "He hardly even jumped for that one."

Scot shook his head. "Just watch him."

"Yeah," Brian said, "especially around LaMoure's cabin!"

They had passed the mill and were nearing LaMoure's cabin when Paint, who was in the lead, stopped of his own accord and snorted at the bushes at the side of the road. Scot shot a warning glance at Jodi.

Suddenly from the bushes leaped three Indian boys. Jodi only caught a glimpse of them before Red reared into the air. This time she was ready for it, and when he came down, she held the reins tightly and tried to calm him with her voice.

"You should know better than that!" Scot was saying angrily to the boys. "Now, go on and leave us alone!"

"You can't make us do nothing," the biggest boy replied defiantly. "You dirty white man! You should get out of here! This is Indian country!" With that, he began whooping and yelling, the other two joining him.

Jodi had her hands full trying to control Red. He lunged, snorted, and fought the bit. Out of the corner of her eye, she saw the big boy lean over and pick up a rock. He pulled back his arm.

"Watch out, Sis!" she heard Brian yell.

She glanced at the boy just as he let the rock fly. "Why, you—" she began, but Red let out a squeal and she felt his muscles tense beneath her.

She realized too late that the moment she had been distracted he had got his head down. The rest was a blur. She felt the horse leap into the air, and then she was flying. She landed with a thud and everything went black.

Jodi opened her eyes, and the world, with Scot's face in the very center, was spinning around. She closed her eyes and moaned.

"Jodi!" he said. His voice sounded frightened. She opened her eyes again, and the world was in its proper place. Beyond Scot's cowboy hat were blue sky and fluffy clouds.

She licked her lips. "I—I guess Red got the best of me," she said shakily.

"Are you all right?" Scot asked. "Is anything broken? Brian went after those boys, but I'm afraid they got away."

She sat up slowly and moved her legs, arms, and hands. She smiled ruefully at Scot.

"Everything's in working order, I guess," she said. "It's a good thing he threw me up here on the bank. I don't think I'd want to land on that hard road." He pulled her to her feet and stood there, holding her hands and looking at her anxiously.

"Are you *sure* you're all right?" he asked.

She pulled her hands away, feeling her face redden. "I'm OK," she replied, walking over to Red and picking up the reins. "I don't want to, but I've got to get back on him and show him who's boss." She mounted, tense and ready, but he merely tossed his head and shifted his feet.

Brian rejoined them and said the boys had got away in the woods.

MaryAnn and Dawn were at the corral when they rode in.

"Where have you guys been?" Dawn asked.

Scot dismounted and opened the gate. "We went down to the store. I wanted to show Jodi LaMoure's place. On the way back, some Indian boys spooked Red, and Jodi got bucked off."

MaryAnn gasped. "Jodi! Are you all right?" She pushed back her long, dark hair.

"I'm OK," Jodi said briefly. "Probably be sore tomorrow. But, boy! Those kids are going to get it if I ever catch them! They did that on purpose, Scot." She unsaddled Red and took off his bridle.

Scot nodded, removed his cowboy hat, and wiped his forehead.

"I'm sure they did it on purpose. I think they were put up to it by someone else."

"But how does this all fit in with Evangeline's step-father disappearing?" Jodi asked.

"What are you guys talking about?" MaryAnn wanted to know. She opened the door of the small shed as Jodi carried in the tack. Scot told them what had happened that morning, and MaryAnn sighed.

"It's all too deep for me," she said. "Come on, Jodi, let's get our things out of that cabin."

"Wait a minute," Jodi said thoughtfully. "What if that person comes back tonight to scare us again. If we set a trap, we might catch him!"

Scot's blue eyes sparkled with interest. "Yeah! You girls can pretend to go to the cabin to sleep, and then when it's dark, sneak out, and Brian and I can sneak in. I have a set of two-way radios, so if something happens, I can call you. We ought to be able to catch them between the five of us."

"Four, you mean," MaryAnn said suddenly. "What if he has a gun? No, thanks! I'm not chasing some guy through the woods at night!"

Scot laughed. "You may not be brave, MaryAnn, but you're sure honest! I'll tell you what. I'll let Mom know what's going on. If she thinks it's too dangerous, we won't do it."

Mrs. Meyer was fixing lunch when they trooped into the kitchen. She smiled at them, and Jodi noticed how pale her face was.

"Mom! You go lie down," Dawn said. "We can get our own lunch." Mrs. Meyer went to lie down on the couch in the living room. Scot approached her and told her all that had happened and what they wanted to do that night.

She thought for some time, and then sighed. "Well, I guess it's OK. But, listen. Call Bob Williams and let him know. If you need him, he can come over, I'm sure."

Scot went to phone, and MaryAnn pulled Jodi to one side.

"Really, Jodi," she said, her brown eyes wide, "I don't want to do it. Who is Bob Williams, anyway?"

"He's another missionary who lives about twenty miles away," Jodi replied. "He's working on translating the Chilcotin language. MaryAnn, you don't have to do anything! The prowler may not even come tonight!"

At dusk, Jodi, MaryAnn, and Dawn chattered noisily as they walked the path to the cabin. But underneath the boisterous words and laughter, Jodi felt prickly with fear. Shivers slipped up and down her spine as she glanced nervously into the dark woods on each side of the trail. Was someone in there, spying on them?

In the cabin, she rolled up her sleeping bag and then sat down to wait for darkness to fall. Finally, at eight o'clock, she stood and motioned to Dawn and MaryAnn.

"OK, let's go," she said in a whisper. "And be quiet! If you hear anything, get into the woods."

One by one, they slipped out into the darkness, leaving a candle burning in the cabin. About twenty steps from the cabin, Jodi paused and looked back. Someone was crossing the trail just behind them! Her heart thumped, and her mouth felt dry. Then she saw two dark shapes creep up to the cabin and go in. She let out a sigh of relief.

"What is it?" MaryAnn whispered, bumping into her.

Jodi gripped her arm. "The boys went into the cabin. Come on!" Slowly they made their way to the house, and then burst into the kitchen, glad to be in the light and warmth of home.

Jodi and MaryAnn went to Scot's room and turned on the two-way radio he had left for them. They looked at the pictures of horses and dogs he had on his walls, the model cars and airplanes, and his shelves of books.

MaryAnn changed into her pajamas and crawled into bed. Jodi lay on top of the covers, fully dressed, and turned off the light. *What a day this has been!* She remembered Evangeline's tragedy, and the concern in Scot's eyes. Did he really like Evangeline? How much? But then she remembered the way he looked at her when she was thrown, and how he held her hands. She sighed, realizing how desperately she wanted him to like her. But Scot was Scot, and you could never tell what was going on inside his head.

She began fighting sleep. She just had to stay awake! But her long lashes drooped, and finally her eyes shut. Suddenly she woke with a start! The radio was buzzing!

She jumped up and grabbed it. "Jodi to Scot," she said into the mouthpiece, and then remembered she had to press the "talk" button.

"Jodi to Scot," she said again. "Do you read me? What's going on?" Static. She tried again, but only heard the same static. She glanced around. What should she do? Wake Dawn and MaryAnn? Call Bob Williams?

But there was no time! She dashed out of the room, stumbled through the dark house, and ran down the trail to the cabin. Just as she neared it, she saw a dark shape run from the back of the cabin and disappear onto the porch.

Without thinking, she ran to the cabin and bounded onto the porch. Suddenly, without warning, someone grabbed her from behind!

3

Trouble for Charlie and Marie

A voice close to her ear called out.

"Hey, Brian! Bring the light! I caught the guy!"

Scot!

A light snapped on at her elbow and Brian's white face was illumined in the glow. "You got someone all right," he said dryly. "You got Jodi!"

"Jodi!" His arms relaxed and she slipped away. "What were you—" He stopped and began chuckling, his brown hair falling on his forehead. At first she was embarrassed and a little angry, but as she thought about it, she began chuckling, too.

"A fine lot of detectives we are," she said, "catching one another! I saw someone run in here, and I had to do something!"

"That was me!" Scot replied. "We heard footsteps again, and Brian buzzed on the radio. Then the guy opened the door, and I yelled from surprise. He took off, and I ran outside to see if I could follow him. But he got away."

Brian yawned. "Well, let's go back to bed."

"I'm going to look for clues," Jodi said, taking the light from his hand and shining it around on the ground. Almost at her feet was a feather. She leaned over to pick it up.

It was broken in the center!

"Hey, what is that?" Brian asked, leaning closer.

"A feather," Scot said, taking it from her hands. "Whoever was in here must have dropped it."

Jodi swallowed hard, fear creeping into her heart. "It's broken, Scot," she said. "I wonder if it's the curse of the broken feather."

Scot looked at her. "You said something like that before. What are you talking about?" His eyes shone in the beam of the flashlight.

She swallowed again. "The day we came," she replied, "I overheard two men talking on the reserve. One of them was the chief. They mentioned something about the curse of the broken feather, and how it was bad news for the reserve. Have you ever heard of it before?"

He shook his head. "No. Never. I wonder—" He stroked the long, gray feather thoughtfully. "Well, let's add this to our collection of clues."

The next morning, Jodi groaned as MaryAnn climbed over her to get out of bed. She pulled the covers over her head and tried to go back to sleep. But soon MaryAnn returned and cheerfully yanked the covers off.

"Come on, sleepyhead," she said. "It's a beautiful day! And we don't want Mrs. Meyer making breakfast for us. I think Scot has already planned all kinds of exciting things to do."

Jodi opened her eyes a slit. "What."

MaryAnn grinned. "You get up, and you'll see," she said and left the room.

Every muscle in Jodi's body screamed as she rolled out of bed and dressed. It felt as if someone had been using her as a punching bag. She limped to the bathroom, washed her face, and frowned at her reflection in the mirror as she tried to make her unruly reddish brown curls behave.

In the kitchen, Dawn was just putting toast and orange juice on a tray for her mother. Jodi frowned.

"Is she still sick?" she asked.

Dawn nodded, tossing back her braids and picking up the tray. "Worse today. She needs lots of rest."

"That's why I've planned a long horseback ride today," Scot said from the table. "We can take our lunch, and give Mom lots of peace and quiet. You girls have to go up Puntzi Mountain before you leave!" He grinned at MaryAnn, who was sitting across the table from him.

Jodi groaned and sat down. "I don't feel like riding anywhere today," she said. "Maybe I'll join your mom in bed."

"OK," MaryAnn replied saucily, "we'll go without you. And maybe even do some investigating on the side!" She grinned mischievously, and Scot winked at her.

Jodi opened her mouth in an angry retort, but then she caught the twinkle in Scot's blue eyes, and she closed her mouth. She knew they were teasing her, but it still hurt. Why couldn't she get a little sympathy?

She frowned at her plate, fighting back the angry thoughts. Dawn put an egg and a piece of toast on her plate and filled her glass with juice.

"Thanks, Dawn," Jodi said, smiling at her. "At least I have one friend left around here!"

"Oh, come on, Jodi," MaryAnn said, giving her shoulder a little shake. "Don't pout. You'll feel better

53

once you get moving around. I'm anxious to see some of this country! Say you'll go with us!"

Jodi smiled. "OK," she said. She glanced at Scot. "Will there be enough horses?"

He nodded. "Evangeline called from the store, and she's coming over. So Dawn can ride with her." He stood and glanced out the window. "Here she is now."

Jodi's heart sank. There was no way she could compete with Evangeline. She picked up her dishes and went to the sink. Scot opened the door and the Indian girl stepped into the kitchen. She wore a bright, blue silky cowboy shirt and as Jodi turned to greet her, she noticed the beaded necklace she wore. It was long, and at the end there was a round circle beaded in blue and white with a black horse's head in the very center. It was a beautiful piece of work, and Jodi found herself wishing she had one like it.

Evangeline seemed very quiet this morning. Her large brown eyes were soft as she glanced around the kitchen. She sat at the table, and when Dawn offered her some breakfast, she nodded and smiled.

Jodi ran some water for the dishes.

"How are you doing, Evangeline?" Scot asked her. Jodi glanced at him. He was sitting next to the girl with his arm draped on the back of her chair. Jodi saw red. She turned back to the dishes and plunged her hands in the hot, soapy water, batting her long lashes to keep back the tears. She clenched her teeth, forgetting Evangeline's terrible problems in the jealousy that flooded her mind. *Why does she always have to butt in?* she thought bitterly.

"OK," Evangeline was saying softly. "But I don't like to put them out, Scot. They don't have much, you know."

"So you just slip away at mealtimes?" Scot asked. "You can't do that! You have to eat, Evangeline, or you'll be getting sick!" His tone sounded as if he were the father, and she, the little girl. Jodi glanced at her and had to admit that she looked very small and vulnerable.

She smiled at Scot. "You know I can't do that," she replied. "I'm OK. Don't worry about me."

Scot shook his head and then stood up. "Let's get going!" he said. "Brian, come with me and we'll saddle the horses. Dawn, you girls can pack the lunch. Hurry!"

Dawn made a face at him. "Yes, Your Highness," she said. But he was already striding through the door.

Jodi finished up the dishes and began making sandwiches.

"Let's make lots," MaryAnn said. Jodi knew she was thinking that if there were any left over, Evangeline could take them for her supper. Suddenly she felt guilty and cheap for the jealous thoughts she had entertained about the Indian girl.

Wrapping the sandwiches reminded her of fixing her school lunches. It had been at lunch hour just last week when she had had that fight with Mona. And she had ended up so angry she could not remember what she had called the other girl. Her cheeks burned at the thought. Was that why Mona had been passing rumors around about her? Maybe it had nothing to do with Ron. But what could she do about it?

MaryAnn's words came back to her. *Forgive her and love her.* She stuffed the sandwiches into the plastic bag and slammed shut a cupboard door. *No way!* There was just no way she could do that!

Evangeline had quietly washed and dried her dishes. Jodi pulled on her cowboy boots and reached for her jacket. Evangeline followed her outside and paused before they went down the hill to the corral, breathing deeply and gazing at the sky.

"It's going to snow," she said matter-of-factly. Jodi looked at her in astonishment.

"In March?" she asked.

Evangeline smiled gently, and Jodi marveled again at her beauty. And there was something else about her that seemed in tune with the living, breathing world of nature around them.

"In March," Evangeline said briefly, and led the way down to the corral. Jodi followed her, and after Jodi came Dawn and MaryAnn, carrying the sandwiches in one bag and a large thermos of water and cookies in another bag.

"Do you want Red again?" Scot asked her as she stepped into the corral.

She nodded. "Sure. He'll be a good saddle horse by the time I go home." For once, she caught him off guard. He laughed and turned to stow the lunch in the saddle bags on his saddle. MaryAnn got on Buckskin, Dawn crawled up on Thunder behind Evangeline, and Scot and Brian mounted Paint.

Scot led the way up a small, rutted road that quickly dwindled to a trail. Red seemed quiet now that he was away from the noisy road and in company with the other horses. Jodi relaxed in the saddle, surprised at how quickly her sore muscles had recovered.

Not far from the Meyers' house, they passed a small cabin set along the trail. There were two horses in a small corral in the back, and all kinds of equipment scattered around the place. A dog began yapping at them, and old Hercules stepped from the open cabin door to survey them with dark, brooding eyes.

"Good morning!" Scot called and waved his hand.

The old man grunted and nodded his head, but he did not smile. Jodi was suddenly struck with an idea. She turned Red to approach the man.

"Hi," she said uncertainly. Now that she was face to face with him, she was not sure what to say. "We—we were just wondering what is the best way up Puntzi Mountain." She glanced at Scot, who had halted Paint down the trail a ways and was looking at her with a puzzled frown.

The old man spit noisily to the side and then fixed Jodi with his beady eyes.

"Thet kid'll know," he croaked, frowning. "Don't come around here botherin' me." He turned and stepped back into the cabin.

Jodi bit her lip. She still had not accomplished what she had set out to do. She dismounted and stepped up to the doorway of the cabin.

"Uh, Mr. Hercules," she called in after him. "I—uh—I heard you were a good trapper. I was wondering if I could see some of your pelts."

The old man returned to the doorway and stared at

57

her. Finally he grunted something unintelligible and disappeared into the cabin.

"Jodi! What are you doing?" Scot called to her impatiently. "Come on!"

Jodi shook her head and waved for him to go on. But he turned Paint around and came back to her. Just then the old man returned, carrying several beaver, muskrat, and coyote pelts.

"Here!" he said, shortly, thrusting them toward Jodi. "This is just a few. Git a good price for them coyote ones."

Jodi reached out and touched the soft fur, her mind racing. How could she find out what she wanted to know? She glanced behind the old man into the dark interior of the cabin. She could see a woodstove, clothes on nails in the wall, and junk on the floor. Finally she handed the pelts back to him and mounted Red.

"Thanks, Mr. Hercules," she said, smiling. "I've never seen such beautiful hides. Maybe I can come some other time and see the rest that you have."

Hercules gave her a smile that revealed dark, tobacco-stained teeth.

"Sure!" he said. "Come any time!"

She turned Red and followed Scot back to the others.

"What in the world!" MaryAnn exclaimed. "Why did you do that, Jodi?" They started out again up the trail.

Scot shook his head. "She sure has a way with him! I've never seen him so friendly!"

"I was just interested in things that are important to him," Jodi replied. "Besides, I wanted to find out something." She glanced at Scot.

"I know," Scot said, grinning at her. "You wanted to find out if he smokes Camels. Am I right?"

Jodi smiled. "Something like that, I guess. But I didn't find out. I guess I'll have to come back."

"Not by yourself!" Scot said sharply. "I don't trust him very far."

Jodi smiled to herself and patted Red. She looked around. They were riding through miles of open country with meadows and stands of trees, splashing through creeks, and catching an occasional glimpse of rabbits, squirrels, and even the flash of a deer jumping through the woods.

Puntzi Mountain rose gradually, and she could feel the horse's muscles pull as they climbed higher. Finally they reached the summit, and she gazed out over the vast wilderness below her—lakes sparkling in the distance, rolling stands of trees, lush meadows, and an occasional Indian cabin.

They dismounted and loosened the cinches of the saddles. Jodi walked around, filling her lungs deeply with the fresh breeze that ruffled her curls. Then she glanced around. Where were the others? Dawn and MaryAnn were on the other side of the summit. Scot and Evangeline had climbed up on a huge rock that was poised on the edge of a sharp drop-off.

Brian walked to the horses. "Come on," he called to Jodi. "Let's eat! I'm starved!" He got the sandwiches and cookies from Scot's saddle bags, and Jodi untied the thermos on the back of MaryAnn's saddle.

"Where are we going to eat?" she asked.

"Up here!" Scot called from the rock.

59

MaryAnn gazed up at him doubtfully. "Is it safe?" she called out.

Both Scot and Evangeline began laughing. "Come on," Scot called back. "It would take an earthquake to dislodge this thing!"

The hastily made, slightly squashed sandwiches were delicious, and Jodi decided it was the fresh air and beautiful surroundings that made them taste so good. After they had eaten, Brian stretched out on the rock and closed his eyes. Evangeline sat cross-legged, gazing at the view meditatively.

"You know," Scot said softly. "There just has to be a Master Designer for nature. You can see God's handiwork in so many things."

Evangeline blinked and glanced at him. "Bert says there is no God," she said slowly. "That God is only a figment of the imagination for weak people who need a crutch." She fell silent.

"And you?" Jodi asked, trying to probe past the stoic stare on her face. "Do you believe there is a god?"

Evangeline took so long in answering that Jodi squirmed and was about to repeat her question, when the girl seemed to come out of some deep reverie. She looked at Jodi and her dark eyes were snapping.

"Of course there's a god," she said scornfully. "Anyone who knows anything about nature must admit to that deep in his heart." She gazed away. Her voice dropped, and her words became sing-song. "The wind, the earth, living things, they speak to me. They tell me of the god of my fathers, the Indian helper-spirits. It is the Indian god I want to worship." She rose suddenly and slid down

60

the rock. Jodi watched as she strode to her horse and tightened the cinch. Dawn made a move as if to get up.

"I'll go talk with her," she said. But Scot laid his hand on her knee.

"No, don't, Dawn. She wants to be alone. I think she'll come back."

Jodi was suddenly tired of Evangeline and her problems. She turned and poked Brian's ribs.

"Hey, you better get up! Didn't I hear you say you wanted to ride back with Dawn?" She flashed him a mischievous grin.

He was up and at her in a second, pinning her arm behind her back and twisting it up. She rose to her knees and in one quick movement twisted her body around and broke his hold.

Dawn laughed. "Oh, that's good, Jodi! Did you see that, Scot?"

Jodi glanced at Scot, but he had been watching Evangeline ride down the hillside. She brushed her hair back and looked away quickly.

"What did I miss?" Scot asked, looking at her.

"Nothing, really," Jodi replied, annoyance creeping into her voice. She rose and brushed off her jeans. "Hadn't we better—" But her words were cut off by the sound of a motor. She glanced around.

"Hey! It's an airplane!" Brian exclaimed, jumping up.

Scot stood to his feet, shielding his eyes as he watched the small blue plane circle not too far away.

"I've never seen that one around here before," he said, "I wonder what they're up to."

"They're landing!" Jodi said, her blue eyes sparkling with excitement. "Look! Right over there in that meadow!" They watched the plane circle lower, dip down, and sink behind a stand of trees.

"Let's go over there," Jodi said. "It's not far."

Scot was already off the rock and striding to his horse. Jodi and the others scrambled down, tightened the cinches, mounted, and followed Scot down off the summit.

As they approached the meadow a little later, Scot pulled Buckskin to a stop behind a fringe of bushes. They dismounted and tied the horses. Jodi could see the small blue plane on the ground now. There were two men standing near it and a pile of boxes at their feet. A black horse stood tied to a group of trees.

"Who is it, Scot?" Jodi asked.

He shook his head. "I can't tell from here. Let's get closer. But stay hidden, and be quiet!" He led the way nearer. Jodi followed close on his heels, careful not to step on twigs and bending over to keep under cover. Finally Scot stopped.

"We better not go any further," he whispered as they huddled close together. Jodi peered through the bushes. They were so close now they could almost hear what the men were saying.

"I know who it is," Dawn whispered. "One of them, anyway. It's Nixon."

Scot nodded. "The other man with the cap must be the pilot."

"Who's Nixon?" Jodi asked. Her nose began itching,

and she rubbed it in alarm. She just could not sneeze now!

"Lyle Nixon," Scot whispered back. "He's assistant to LaMoure at the mill. What's that coming over there?"

Something was coming across the meadow, and as it neared, Jodi could see it was an Indian wagon and horses. The wagon pulled up to the plane and stopped. A wizened little Indian woman sat holding the reins.

"Maggie!" Scot breathed. "What's she doing here?"

Dawn glanced at Jodi. "She lives all by herself up in a meadow not too far away. She's one who has received Christ."

"I wonder what's in the boxes!" MaryAnn whispered, her brown eyes wide.

"It looks like one of your candle-meetings, Scot," Brian remarked.

Scot nodded. "Sure does."

They watched as the two men loaded the boxes into Maggie's wagon. Then she picked up the reins and drove away. Nixon walked to his horse, and the plane taxied over the bumpy meadow grass.

"Let's follow Maggie!" Jodi said eagerly when they got back to their horses.

Scot shook his head. "No, I think we should get home," he said with a worried frown. "I shouldn't have left Mom alone so long as it is."

Jodi frowned and almost turned Red to follow Maggie by herself. But then she realized she could not find her way home. Feeling frustrated and impatient, she turned to follow behind Buckskin. What did that planeload of boxes have to do with the mystery? Or did it have anything at all to do with it? She sighed and rubbed her forehead.

Evangeline did not appear again, and Scot said she must have gone home. They rode the horses into the corral and unsaddled them. Jodi trudged tiredly up the hill to the house. Mrs. Meyer was in the living room, dressed and studying a flannelgraph.

She glanced up as they came in. "Oh! You're back. I'm feeling better, so I thought we'd have our little meeting tonight." She glanced at Jodi and MaryAnn. "On Wednesday nights we have a service for the Indian people. Scot plays his guitar, and I tell a story when Mr. Meyer isn't here. I'll go down to the reserve and pick up people after supper."

Scot frowned. "If anyone will come!"

The smile faded from his mother's face, and her eyes darkened. "Let's just pray they do," she said in a low voice.

But that night, when she pulled up to the small frame building they used for the chapel, there were only two people in the van.

"Is that all?" Scot asked as the young couple, Charlie and Marie, stepped into the building.

Mrs. Meyer frowned. "I'm afraid so," she said in a whisper. "Even the children ran away when I drove up. Every door on the reserve was closed. I just don't understand it!"

Jodi felt the goosebumps rise on her arms. Was it the chief, Felix Dennis, who was turning his people against the white man? Or was it someone else, someone even more sinister and evil? A feeling of dread crept over her.

She and the others rode along with Mrs. Meyer when she took Charlie and Marie home. The door of their small house stood ajar when they arrived, and Jodi saw that the two front windows were broken. Charlie leaped out of the van, followed by Mrs. Meyer and Scot. Marie's fingers shook as she picked up the baby basket and headed for the house. Jodi climbed out of the van after her.

Marie stepped into the cabin and cried out. Jodi followed her and gasped. The entire cabin was a disaster!

4

What Was in the Boxes

The Indian couple stared at the mess in quiet despair. It was true that they had nothing fancy or really very valuable. But it was their home, and now everything was ruined. Marie set the baby basket down and picked up a broken plate. Then she let it drop out of her fingers and smash on the floor.

Scot was on his knees, trying to fix the broken legs on the table. Charlie placed his hand on his shoulder and shook his head sadly.

"It's no use, Scot," he said. He paced to stare out the broken window. "Who would do this?" he asked himself quietly. "I've got no enemies. Unless it's—" His brown eyes glinted, and he shut his mouth in a tight line.

Mrs. Meyer shook her head. "This is terrible! Scot and my husband can help fix things later, but in the meantime, you can't stay here. Why don't you get your clothes together and come up to the guest cottage by our house? We have everything in there you'll need. OK?"

Charlie nodded. "OK."

Suddenly Scot leaped to his feet and glanced around.

"Hey! Where's Evangeline? I thought she was staying with you, Charlie!"

Charlie shook his head. "No, she isn't. I think she's still in the cabin Bert Leech was in. I saw her going in there the other day." He turned to gather up their few belongings and food.

Scot dashed out the door. Jodi stepped to the doorway and gazed out into the night, feeling a little sick. Who would do this? She felt sure Charlie knew, but he would not talk. That was the Indian way. She glanced down. What was that?

Slowly she leaned over and picked up a long, grey feather, broken in the center! Her mind whirled as she stroked it. Was this some kind of a sign? She carried it inside and showed it to Charlie.

"I found this on your doorstep," she said, handing it to him.

His eyes widened and he stepped back. "No!" he said, terrified. "Take it away! Get it out of here!"

Jodi was too startled to move for a second, and then she quickly walked to the door and threw it outside.

"What does the feather mean?" Brian asked.

Charlie grunted. "I don't know," he said. Jodi sighed. He would not talk about that, either. What did it mean? Why was he so afraid of the broken feather? She swallowed, fear creeping into her heart.

She went outside and stood by the van. Scot appeared out of the darkness.

"Did you find Evangeline?" she asked.

He shook his head. "No. She isn't in the cabin Leech was in. But it looks like she may be coming back for food. I wonder where she is! She can't live like this!"

Jodi glanced around. "I don't know, Scot," she said wearily. Mrs. Meyer, Charlie, Marie, and the others

67

came out of the cabin carrying boxes and bags. They put their things in the van and got in.

At the house, after they had settled Charlie and Marie, Jodi saw Scot sneak out the door. She grabbed her jacket and followed him. He turned when he heard the door shut.

"Where are you going?" Jodi asked as she approached him in the dark.

He turned to the trail that led to the corral. "Just a hunch," he said, leading the way down the hill. "Now be quiet!"

He shone his light into the corral. There was Red, Paint, and Buckskin. A dark shadow in the far corner lifted its head. *Thunder!* Jodi gasped. What was he doing here? Scot turned and walked to the small shed. He opened the door and flashed the light around inside.

Jodi heard a low cry and peered from behind him. Evangeline was sitting up, shielding her eyes from the light. Underneath her was a saddle blanket, and she had an old coat thrown over her.

"OK," Scot said, turning the light from her eyes. "Come on up to the house. Why did you hide out in there?"

The slender girl stood up. "I—I was staying at Bert's cabin, but I don't want to anymore. Then when I heard what happened to Charlie and Marie—"

"How did you know?" Jodi cut in.

"I was sleeping in your small cabin first," Evangeline explained while Scot led the way up the hill. "When I heard you coming, I slipped outside and overheard you talking. Then I came down here."

68

"Well, you're not sleeping in that shed tonight!" Scot said as he held the door for them to go in the house. "Mom! We have another guest!"

The next morning when MaryAnn shook her awake, Jodi rolled over and groaned. She had been wrestling with someone all night, it seemed, and her mind and body were tired. She looked at the calendar on the wall. Thursday. They were going home Saturday, and she had made no progress on this terrible, baffling mystery! A sense of urgency pressed upon her as she thought of the Meyers' deadline approaching, Evangeline's missing stepfather, and the trouble that Charlie and Marie were experiencing.

She got out of bed and began dressing slowly. The clues lay on Scot's desk. The note they found beside the cabin, a broken feather, a half-smoked Camel cigarette. Not really very much to go on. She ticked off the suspects in her mind. Hercules, LaMoure, Nixon, and Felix Dennis, the chief. Or were they all working together? Why did anyone want the Meyers out?

She sighed. What could she do? And then she remembered Scot's words the day they went to the store. It was after they had passed LaMoure's cabin. *If you want to look for clues,* he had said, *this would be a good place to start.*

Right then she decided to do some investigating that morning after breakfast. In the kitchen, she found Dawn and MaryAnn at the table, but Scot and Evangeline were gone.

"Where's Scot?" she asked as she poured herself some dry cereal.

Dawn pointed outside. "Seeing Evangeline off. She wanted to go back to the reserve before anyone found out she was here. I'll get you some juice."

Jodi ate the cereal and drank the juice quickly. Then she threw on her jacket and stepped outside. Just around the corner of the house, she heard voices. She stopped.

"I'll be all right," a girl said, and she realized it was Evangeline. "If I need help, I'll call or try to get over here. Thanks, Scot, for everything."

Not wanting to eavesdrop, she stepped around the corner of the house. What she saw made her freeze to the spot. Evangeline had reached over to Scot and was hugging him! She whirled and ran back around the house, holding her burning face in her hands. Tears stung her eyes, and she wiped them away.

"What's the matter?" Brian came up behind her. He was grinning. "Can't you stand a little competition, Jodi?"

She whirled to him, her anger rising suddenly and hot.

"It's none of your business!" she heard herself screaming. "I wish you'd never come! You're just stupid! You don't know anything, so stay out—" She stopped, hearing steps coming up behind. In a flash, she knew it was Scot and that he had heard every word of her outburst.

She ran into the house, slammed the door, tore through the kitchen, into Scot's room, and flung herself on the bed, crying into the pillow. When the crying stopped, she reached onto the bedstand for a Kleenex and saw Scot's Bible. She sat, looking at it, dabbing her nose and wiping her eyes. How long had it been since she had read her

70

Bible? *Too long,* she thought as she dug in her suitcase to find it.

She flipped open the pages and found herself in the book of Ephesians, the fourth chapter. She read through the chapter and then stopped abruptly on the last two verses. The searing pain of guilt pierced her. She read them over again slowly.

"Let all bitterness, and wrath, and anger, and clamour, and evil speaking, be put away from you, with all malice: and be ye kind one to another, tenderhearted, forgiving one another even as God for Christ's sake hath forgiven you."

Tears stung her eyes once more. Oh, how bitter and angry she had been! And unforgiving! "Oh, Lord, I'm sorry I've been so angry and bitter. I know I can't control my temper unless You help me, so please help me!"

When she went into the kitchen she found that Brian and Scot had gone fishing. MaryAnn was strumming on Scot's guitar in the living room, so Jodi went in and sat beside her on the couch.

"Where's Mrs. Meyer?" she asked. "Not feeling well again?"

MaryAnn shook her head. "She tried to do too much last night, I guess." She pushed back her hair. "Is something wrong, Jodi? It looks like you've been crying."

Jodi leaned back on the couch. "A whole lot is bothering me, MaryAnn. That Evangeline, for one thing! I bet she's a spy! And she's playing dirty. I saw her hugging Scot!"

MaryAnn smiled and strummed on the guitar. "So that's it."

71

"No, that's not it!" Jodi sat up. "Not all of it, anyway. I'm really concerned about this mystery. And I wish I could do something! Hey, MaryAnn, let's go riding!"

MaryAnn put the guitar down and eyed her suspiciously. "Just what do you have in mind?"

Jodi grinned. "Just a little investigating. Come on, OK?"

Scot and Brian had taken Paint and Buckskin, and MaryAnn was hesitant to ride double on Red.

"Come on," Jodi coaxed. "I've got a good hold on him. Just slip on from the fence, OK?"

Red pranced a little when he felt MaryAnn's weight behind the saddle, but Jodi held him in tight, and soon they were on the road, headed for LaMoure's cabin.

"We should get off the road before we get to his cabin," Jodi remarked, studying the woods on the side of the road. "Here's a trail going in." She turned Red off the road, and when they could see the top of LaMoure's cabin, she stopped and they got off.

"Let's hope the dogs are asleep," Jodi whispered as they began creeping closer to the buildings.

MaryAnn drew back. "Oh, Jodi! The dogs! They'll give us away for sure. Let's get out of here now!"

"Come on," Jodi said, pulling her along. "Maybe they're asleep."

Cautiously she approached the cabin, and finally she stopped behind a shed. There was a lot of junk around, and two trucks parked in front of the cabin. She peered around, and then ducked back. The cabin door had slammed!

MaryAnn was ready to run, but Jodi pulled her down

72

and put her finger to her lips. Some men were talking. If only she could hear what they said! And then one of the men yelled loudly.

"I want them out! I don't care what it takes!"

Jodi gripped MaryAnn's arm, her blue eyes wide and her heart pounding. Who had said that? If she could only see! Slowly she peeked around the shed. There were three big barrels between the cabin and the shed. Still holding MaryAnn's arm, she crept up behind the barrels, and peered around them. A girl came from the cabin and got on a black horse that was tied nearby. Jodi gasped. *Evangeline!* What was she doing here?

At the same time, one man had gotten in the truck and was backing it away. Who was it? She could not tell. The other man must have gone back into the cabin. But no! Someone was coming closer! She scrunched down beside MaryAnn and held her breath as the steps neared. There was the sound of a key being inserted in a lock, and then a door opening. The man was going in the shed!

MaryAnn put her mouth on Jodi's ear. "Let's get out of here now!" she hissed.

Just then the man came out and walked away. Jodi nodded. It was too dangerous for them to be here. Slowly she stood up and began edging away from the barrels. They were a few steps from the shed door when she heard a truck approaching the driveway. They were going to be caught out in the open!

Where could they go? She glanced around and saw the open door of the shed. Quickly she dashed in and pulled MaryAnn after her. The truck turned into the driveway and pulled up to the cabin. They heard a man get out and go into the house.

"Whew! That was close!" Jodi sighed, sinking down on a box in the cluttered shed.

"Come on, Jodi!" MaryAnn cried. "Let's get out of here! What if that man comes back! There's no place to hide in here!"

Jodi glanced around. That was true! She stood up and looked at the box she had been sitting on.

"MaryAnn!" she said, grabbing her arm. "I wonder if these are the boxes that came on the plane!" She stepped over to one that was partly open.

Overcome with curiosity, she lifted off the slats. Crumpled newspaper! What was under that? She reached under the paper and felt something cold and hard. With one frantic movement she flung off the newspapers and gasped.

Nestled there in a bed of newspaper packing lay a wicked looking shotgun.

5

Red Dog Devil

Jodi's hands shook as she replaced the newspapers and the slats on the box. What did that mean? MaryAnn pulled her from the shed, but just as they stepped outside, the cabin door slammed again. Someone was coming!

Jodi whirled to run, but she tripped over some cans on the ground, and fell. The racket brought the dogs and the man on the run.

"Hey! You kids!" he yelled.

Jodi urged MaryAnn on. "Go on! I'll get out of this somehow!" MaryAnn needed no second invitation. Hair flying, she soon disappeared into the trees just as the man descended on Jodi.

It was Lyle Nixon. He grabbed her arm as she scrambled to her feet. He was short and wiry, with an unshaven face and dark, beady eyes.

"Come on, kid. I'm showing you to the boss," he sneered, beginning to drag her along. For a few seconds, she gave in to him, remembering her self-defense training. Then the moment she had been waiting for came.

"You dogs, get!" Nixon kicked at one of the dogs, momentarily loosening his hold on her arm. That was all she needed. She twisted out of his grasp, turned, and ran to the woods. MaryAnn was holding Red, and looked relieved to see her coming. They mounted, and once on the road, Jodi kicked the horse to a fast gallop.

"Guns!" Mrs. Meyer repeated a little later as Jodi finished relating to her what had happened. She was snuggled under the covers in her bedroom. It was a cozy room with a patchwork quilt on the bed, hooked rugs on the floor, and an old-fashioned lamp on the bedstand. Just now it smelled of Vicks and camphor oil, and Jodi noticed steam shooting from a vaporizer near the bed.

"Oh, I wish John would come home," Mrs. Meyer was saying as she slowly got out of bed and pulled on her robe. "I guess I should call the police. I'll report Evangeline's missing stepfather, too." She shook her head and passed her hand over her forehead.

Jodi and MaryAnn followed her to the living room where she sat in the large chair and lifted the receiver from the telephone on the end table. Dawn came in with a pile of clothes she had just removed from the line. Jodi sat beside her on the couch and helped fold them. Mary-Ann told her what had just happened.

"The closest detachment is forty miles away," Dawn said. "They have to cover hundreds of square miles."

Mrs. Meyer replaced the receiver. "There are some officers coming through here later today," she said. "They'll stop in and do some questioning." She rose wearily and went back to her bedroom.

Jodi heard the kitchen door slam. She turned away from the living room door and became very busy folding clothes as Scot and Brian tromped in. Scot sprawled tiredly on the big chair, and Brian flopped down on the oval braided rug on the floor.

"Any luck?" MaryAnn asked, glancing over at Scot. He shook his head and picked up his guitar. Jodi stole a look at him. What would he think of her now? She glanced at Brian and caught his eye. Dropping the socks she was mating, she stood and grabbed him by the arm, towing him along with her to the kitchen.

"Let me go!" he said angrily, pulling away from her.

Jodi swallowed. "I'm sorry I yelled at you, Brian," she said softly.

"It's OK," he replied quickly. "Just leave me out of your fight over Scot." He grinned at her.

She frowned. "I think the fight has been won," she said. "I don't care, anyway."

"Don't be so sure," Brian countered. "Scot told me something—" He broke off and smiled at her.

"What!" she demanded, grabbing his arm.

He started laughing. "I can't tell you! Honest, Jodi! But—but it's good!" The last came out as she tickled his ribs, and he collapsed on the floor, giggling.

She grinned and helped him to his feet, mussing up his hair. *Maybe it isn't such a bad thing having a little brother,* she thought. *In fact, it's pretty nice!*

MaryAnn was just finishing the story of their morning adventures, and Jodi sat down beside Dawn, hiding behind her so Scot would not see her face.

But he would not leave her alone. He got up from the chair and came over to sit beside her on the couch.

"How'd you get away from Nixon?" he asked. She looked at him and his clear, blue eyes held hers, telling her it was OK.

She flushed and looked down. "I—I just twisted around and broke his hold. I've been learning things like that in a self-defense class at school."

77

He smiled. "That's great! But I wonder why they had guns in the shed!"

"Yeah, and I saw Evangeline there, too," Jodi exclaimed. "She came out of LaMoure's cabin and got on Thunder and rode away."

A puzzled frown played on Scot's forehead as he thought about that piece of information. He opened his mouth to comment, but the dogs began barking outside, and a wagon pulled by two horses rattled by the window.

"Hey, that's Maggie!" Dawn said. "I wonder what she wants!" They all stood and went to the kitchen where Scot opened the door.

Maggie came inside and sat at the table, her bright eyes following Dawn around as she made her some strong tea. Jodi sat across the table from her, and the others sat down, too.

"Down from the meadow, huh?" Scot said. "Maybe you go shopping?"

Maggie grinned toothlessly and nodded her head. "Maybe," she said.

"Maggie," Jodi began uncertainly, "I see you in a meadow the other day."

The old woman smiled and nodded.

"Airplane there, too," she continued. "Men put boxes on your wagon. You drive off with them."

Maggie smiled again, but she looked down at the floor and began tying the laces on her moccasin.

"I wonder, why is she taking boxes away? Who talk to you, Maggie? Who tell you to do that?" Jodi paused but the woman did not seem to be listening.

Scot leaned toward her. "Do you know, Maggie?"

78

Maggie straightened up, smiling. "White man, he tell me to take boxes. He pay me money!" She patted a worn leather pouch slung over her shoulder. "Lots of money, if I don't ask question. Just take boxes away. So I said yes! Maggie haul boxes away!" She took a slurpy drink of tea. "I ask no question. I got money."

Jodi sighed. She knew it was useless to ask any more questions. After Maggie left, Scot had an idea.

"Let's ride down by the store and see if we can find out anything," he said. "And I'd like to stake out La-Moure's cabin. At a safe distance, of course!" He grinned at Jodi.

MaryAnn waved her hand. "You guys go ahead. I've had enough adventures for one day. I want to do some reading, and maybe I'll bake something for dessert tonight."

"I'll stay and help," Dawn offered, a little reluctantly.

"No you won't," Jodi put in, pulling her toward the door. "When MaryAnn reads, you might as well be in the next country. Come on, we may need another detective."

As they walked to the corral, Jodi felt strange, as if someone was watching her. She glanced up the hill into the woods and caught a movement among the trees. Was someone spying on them? She shivered, and strode to the shed, picking up Red's bridle.

"I think someone's up there in the woods," she said to Scot as he gathered up a saddle. "Do you think someone's spying on us?"

Scot dropped the saddle and dashed out the door. Jodi watched as he sprinted up the hill and disappeared among the trees. A few minutes later, he returned.

"I caught a glimpse of someone," he muttered as he picked up the saddle, "but that's all. Could have been an Indian kid."

Jodi frowned. *Someone must be spying on us,* she thought. *How did anyone know we were staying in the cabin that night?* She finished saddling Red and then walked up in the trees on the hillside, studying the ground.

"Jodi, come on!" Brian called.

She penetrated the woods a little deeper, her eyes still on the ground. Suddenly she stopped and leaned over, her hand shaking as she picked something up from the ground. The butt of a cigarette! She studied it, her heart thumping. *A Camel!* Quickly she turned and ran back down the hill. Scot and Brian sat on Paint, and Dawn watched her from Buckskin.

"Look!" Jodi panted. "I found this up there! It's still warm, too!" She handed the cigarette to Scot, who studied it and then put it in his pocket.

At the store, Jodi halted Red and pointed to a stand of trees behind the building.

"Let's tie the horses back there," she said to Scot.

Scot tipped his cowboy hat at her. "OK, Sherlock," he said, leading the way into the trees. They dismounted and wandered toward the small store.

"Listen!" Jodi said, glancing around at the trucks, the garage off to one side where several men gathered around disabled cars, and the gas pumps. "You boys case the joint out here. Just wander around and see if you can pick up any interesting talk. Dawn and I will wander around inside, OK?"

Scot was already walking listlessly to the garage. Jodi turned to step inside the back door of the store, but Dawn hesitated.

"Come on," Jodi said, pulling on her arm.

Dawn was looking over at some small cabins near the store.

"Jodi!" she exclaimed. "I saw someone in that cabin!" She pointed. All of the four cabins seemed vacant.

Jodi caught her breath. A rather large man appeared for a moment in the doorway of one cabin, and then disappeared.

"Leech!" Dawn gasped. "That was Bert Leech, Jodi!"

She stared at the cabin, but there was nothing more to be seen. She squeezed Dawn's arm.

"Then he isn't missing," she murmured slowly. "I wonder what he's up to." She turned into the store and headed toward the front counter. Dawn told her that the lady running the cash register was the owner.

On the way she picked up a package of gum.

"Hi," she said to the woman who was punching keys on the rickety old cash register. "I was wondering if you are renting out those cabins in the back."

The woman pushed her straggily brown hair from her face.

"Sure, we rent them," she said briskly. "If anyone wants them. It's sort of off-season now." She turned to the next customer, an older Indian man.

"But do you have anyone in them now?" Jodi persisted.

The woman glanced at her sharply. "No, I don't. But I just gave a key to someone who might rent one. I don't think it's your business, though." She turned and began boxing up some groceries.

Jodi and Dawn stepped outside.

"She sure got unfriendly when you asked about the cabins," Dawn said.

Jodi nodded. "Something's going on here. Let's find the boys." Scot and Brian were around back with the horses.

"What did you find out?" Jodi asked Scot.

He shook his head and grinned. "That it will take two weeks to fix Tommy Dennis's wreck, that Frank drove off the road last night, and various other tidbits that I don't think you'd be interested in."

"Scot!" Dawn exploded. "We saw Leech! Over there in that cabin! And the owner said she gave the key to someone who might rent it!"

Scot did not seem surprised, only puzzled. "He must be hiding out," he said. "I wonder why."

"Maybe he's in danger," Brian suggested as they mounted and trotted out to the road. "Maybe he's hiding from whoever would be after him."

Scot rubbed his forehead. "It just doesn't add up," he said thoughtfully. "But let's get on over to LaMoure's." They rode for some time, and then he slowed Paint and glanced at Jodi as she rode closer on Red.

"Hey, why don't you and Dawn go over to Nixon's," he said. "Just do the same as what we're going to do here. Position yourselves somewhere safe and watch the cabin to see who comes and goes." He paused and dug in his saddle bag.

"Here," he said, handing her the two-way radio. "I've

got the other one. If you need help, call us." He turned Paint into the woods.

"Where is Nixon's?" Jodi asked Dawn as they went on down the road.

"A little further on, past where our road turns off," Dawn said, motioning on down the road. They trotted past LaMoure's cabin, and Jodi studied it out of the corner of her eye. There were several trucks around, but no one was in sight.

A while later, Dawn pulled back on Buckskin. "I think his cabin is just around that bend, Jodi," she said. "What do we do now?" She tossed her braids behind her shoulders.

"Let's go into the woods and sneak up behind the cabin," Jodi replied, turning Red off the road. "Maybe we can climb a tree or something." She led the way into the woods and rode until she could see the top of Nixon's cabin. They dismounted and tied the horses to the trees.

She nodded toward a large pine tree not far away. Then, grasping the two-way radio, she crept through the woods with Dawn at her heels. Finally they reached the tree and climbed up into the lower branches.

"Are you OK?" she asked Dawn. The other girl nodded, and they both looked at the cabin. It was a small rough-boarded cabin, with a battered red truck parked outside and two sleeping dogs by the front door.

Suddenly they heard the sound of a motor in the distance. A truck was coming! Jodi tensed, wondering if it would turn out to be Nixon's. It was a four-wheel drive police vehicle.

She watched it fly on down the road, her heart beating hard.

"We should be home to talk with them!" she said to Dawn. She turned on the radio to call the boys and tell them they were going home. Her finger moved to push the "talk" button, but before she did, the radio crackled and a man's voice boomed out at her.

She almost dropped the radio in her surprise, but she gripped it hard and listened.

"Red Dog Devil," the man's voice grated out, "Red Dog Devil. Over." The voice paused and she could not hear the other side of the conversation. She glanced at Dawn. "Got it on, Boss," the voice continued. "It'll drive them out, I'm sure. If it doesn't, we'll burn 'em out! Over and out."

Jodi sat there, staring at the radio in her hand, frozen by fear. *Red Dog Devil must be a code name,* she thought. *But what did they mean by burning?*

"We better get home!" Dawn said, her eyes wide.

Jodi pushed the "talk" button. "I'll call the boys first," she said. But Dawn reached over and stopped her.

"No!" she said. "Jodi, if you can hear them, they'll be able to hear you!"

Jodi scrambled down from the tree and led the way to the horses.

"OK then," she said to Dawn. "You go back to La-Moure's and tell the boys. I'll go on home and talk with the police."

In a flurry of dust, she rode up to the corral a little later and unsaddled Red, turning him loose. Then she dashed up to the house, and was just reaching for the door when she stopped. Something was tacked to the door!

84

It was a plain white envelope. *Who put it here?* Her fingers shook as she tore the envelope from the door and entered the kitchen. Mrs. Meyer, still in her robe, was poring over a cookbook with MaryAnn at the table. They both looked up, startled, when she burst in.

"I've got to talk to the police!" she said. "I just heard something over the two-way radio about burning this place!" She paused for breath and crumpled into a chair.

Mrs. Meyer shook her head, her blue eyes dark with worry. "They were just here ten minutes ago. You should have seen them on the road."

Jodi rubbed her forehead. "Well, I didn't. Maybe Scot and Brian will see them. Here, I found this on the door." She shoved the white envelope toward Mrs. Meyer.

Mrs. Meyer brushed back her short dark hair. She picked up the envelope, tore it open, and drew out a white piece of paper. Some ashes fell from the creases of the paper as she unfolded it.

"What in the world!" she said. Jodi leaned closer to see. On the inside of the paper was the rough sketch of a wolf, with words scrawled over it.

Jodi read out loud, fear creeping over her as she read.

"Curse of the wolf. On this house. Ashes of his hair. You must leave. Do not look back." She collapsed back into her chair, her heart pounding in her ribs and her blue eyes wide with stark fear.

"What—what does it mean?" she asked.

Mrs. Meyer's mouth was set in a firm line. "It's a curse," she said and MaryAnn gasped. "Someone's using the witchdoctor."

"What are we going to do?" MaryAnn cried.

"Burn this letter and bury everything outside," Mrs. Meyer replied as she scooped up the ashes, reached for a box of matches, and nearly ran outside. Jodi watched from the window as she burned it and then quickly dug a hole and buried the ashes.

Just then Scot, Brian, and Dawn came up the hill from the corral. Jodi saw them stop and talk to Mrs. Meyer. Then they all trudged into the kitchen.

"Did you talk to the police?" Jodi asked Scot at once.

He shook his head and removed his cowboy hat. His face, usually so full of life and fun, was pale, and there was fear in his eyes. Had he given up hope? Suddenly she wanted to say something that would snap him out of his despondency.

"What did you see at LaMoure's?" she asked him as he got a drink of water. She hurried on without letting him answer. "We heard someone over the radio, Scot. They were talking about burning!"

He shook his head and sat down at the table, not looking at her. "I know," he said slowly. "Dawn told me. The police stopped at LaMoure's, but they only talked with him for a short while and then left." He paused. "I don't know—I just feel like giving up."

Jodi sighed and sat down at the far end of the table, holding her face in her hands. If Scot felt like quitting, she felt like crying. Everything seemed too big, too scary. And if the police would not even help—

Mrs. Meyer came to the table with her Bible. "Now, listen," she said calmly. "Our enemy uses fear to gain his purposes."

"Enemy," Jodi repeated, glancing at her. "Do you mean the people who are trying to get you to leave?"

Mrs. Meyer shook her head. "No, I'm talking about our *real* enemy—Satan. He is the one who is really behind this, you know. And he delights to put fear into the heart of God's children." She paused, glancing around. "I see it in the eyes of you kids. All right, let's read some of the Bible, and then we'll pray. You know, Proverbs says that a curse causeless shall not land. That means that if we have done nothing to deserve it, the curse will not come to pass."

After the Bible reading and prayer, Jodi went to Scot's room and shut the door. What did it all mean? She sat on the edge of the bed. *Red Dog Devil. That must have referred to this curse. But why? Who was behind it all? Could it be Felix Dennis?*

She rubbed her forehead and thought hard. He had been friendly before, but he was not friendly now. Was someone perverting his thinking and attitude? Who was it? LaMoure? Why would LaMoure want them out? Why was he getting shipments of guns from small airplanes that landed in remote meadows? And how did the old man, Hercules, fit in? Was he picking up money, like Maggie did, to spy on them and run errands?

Suddenly she stood up. There was something she had to do! She strode outside and glanced around. As she began walking up the small rutted road leading to Hercules' cabin, she felt uneasy. Scot had warned her not to go alone. She gripped her hands tightly. *Someone has to do something!* she thought, stamping her foot down hard on the trail. *I'll just have to be careful, that's all!*

87

6

Another Broken Feather

Hercules did not seem to be home. Jodi poked around
the cabin, but even the dog was gone. She knocked at
the tightly closed door, searching the ground. Maybe she
could find something that would give her a clue.

There was plenty of junk, garbage, and old tools lying
around, but there were no Camel cigarette butts. She sat
down on a stump, the sun warm on her back. Suddenly
she felt more discouraged than ever before.

"Huh!" There was a grunt behind her, and she leaped
to her feet and whirled around. The old man had come
up behind her so quietly she had not heard a thing. His
hound flopped on the ground nearby as he stared at her
with his dark, brooding eyes.

"I—I came to see your pelts, Hercules," she stam-
mered, her muscles tense to run at the least sign of danger. "You said I could any time."

"Come on, then," he grunted, turning to go to the front
of the cabin. She followed him and sat on a stump of
wood near the front door.

He rummaged around in his cabin for some time, and
then returned with a pile of soft fur, which he laid on her
lap. He seated himself on a bench he had built to the
cabin wall.

She stroked the furs softly. "Oh, they are beautiful!
What is this one?" She held up a thick reddish colored
pelt.

"That there's a fox," Hercules replied. "It'll bring a top price. Them two are mink, and these are beaver. Git lots of beaver down by the river."

She smiled and put the mink close to her cheek. "I love to feel these furs," she said, "but I'd hate to kill such beautiful animals."

He shifted his legs and let out his breath noisily.

"Just part of the job," he said finally. "Course I hate to see too many animals killed. Some fellars would come in here and try to get rich offen 'em. Me, I just take what I need to live on."

"You—you mean there's poachers in this area?" she asked, gazing at him carefully.

He snorted. "You better believe it, girl!" He leaned forward and pointed at her. "Wherever there's money to be made, you'll find some crook there to git his hands on it."

He leaped up, and she jumped. Agitated, he paced in front of her.

"You may not believe it, but there's some people who would steal a baby's milk to get rich. Why, there's some down at the Indian reserve right now that'd—" He caught himself up short, grunted something in his throat, and sat down again on the bench.

Jodi watched him, wide-eyed, hoping he would continue what he had been saying. Who was at the reserve? What were they doing?

She opened her mouth to ask, but stopped when she saw his hand moving to his shirt pocket. Was he going to smoke? What brand did he use? With bated breath, she watched his hand. It felt around inside his pocket and finally drew something out. *The makings!*

She let out her breath as she watched him expertly roll his own cigarette. Then he was not the spy who had dropped the Camel cigarette butt in the woods! She stood up.

"Thanks for letting me see the pelts, Hercules," she said. "I'd better be going now. Good-bye!"

He nodded and grunted. She took one step away, and then stopped. He was muttering something almost under his breath. She turned and looked at him.

His eyes pierced hers. "There's trouble brewin', youngun," he said softly. "You better watch out!"

For several seconds his eyes bored into hers. Finally she turned away and ran. The fear that crawled upon her lent speed to her feet. Around the bend, through the meadow, under the trees she flew. Finally, her breath coming in gasps and her heart pounding, she stopped beside a small lake.

Flopping down on a log to catch her breath, she gazed out over the tiny lake. It was perfectly still, like a piece of glass reflecting the evergreens that blanketed the hills around and the soft sunset colors of the western sky. She heard a squirrel chattering in a tree nearby, a bee buzzing by, and the rustle of birds in the bushes.

As her heart slowed she began drinking in the beauty all around. Again her eyes rested on the lake. Somewhere, not too long ago, she had heard someone say that Christians should be like mirrors, reflecting the beauty of Christ to the world. And then she remembered the words

90

she had read in the Bible. "Forgiving one another as God for Christ's sake hath forgiven you."

There was one part of her that wanted to follow God and obey His Word, no matter what the cost. But another part of her stood up and demanded her rights. She had a right to the respect of others! Who did Mona think she was, spreading lies about her? And Evangeline—

She sighed, wishing she could become a knob on the log she was sitting on, and not have to face the problems and fears that seemed to overwhelm her at times. She sighed again and stood up.

Dusk was settling over the hills as Jodi approached the house. She clenched her fists as she looked at the house with its bright lights gleaming out into the coming darkness. There just had to be a way to help the Meyers! This light to the Indian people could not die out!

Suddenly the dogs began barking, and a truck roared past her and screeched to a stop beside the house. A small man leaped from the driver's seat and banged on the door.

She hurried up. It was Nixon!

"What do you want?" she asked defensively.

He glared at her. "I want to talk to your mother!" he said.

"She's sick," Scot said behind them, coming up the hill from the corral. "Just tell me." Evangeline was a shadow at his side.

MaryAnn opened the door, and behind her was Dawn. Nixon glanced around impatiently. "All right," he growled. "Just listen, cuz I ain't repeatin' nothin'! I'm gettin' out of here," he declared, motioning to the truck.

For the first time Jodi noticed it was piled high with boxes and furniture.

Nixon's dark eyes glinted. "It's gettin' too hot for me. And it's going to get a lot hotter for you, too! Let me tell you, you better clear out! You guys are closer to heaven than what you think!"

Jodi gasped. Nixon whirled around, leaped into the truck, and roared away. She followed the others into the house where they gathered at the kitchen table.

"What was that all about?" Mrs. Meyer asked, pulling her robe around her as she came into the kitchen.

Scot's eyes flashed as he told her what Nixon had just said.

"Do—do you think he might have been faking it just to scare us?" MaryAnn asked fearfully.

Scot shook his head. "No, he meant it, I'm sure! He was all packed up! Something big is going on!"

Mrs. Meyer nodded. "I'll put a message for Dad on the radio tomorrow morning," she said. "He'll be listening. He might even be on his way home now."

Jodi glanced at Evangeline, who sat next to Scot. Her face was as white as a sheet! Suddenly she groaned softly and then crumpled to the floor!

Scot leaped up and had her in his arms almost before she hit the floor. He carried her into the living room and laid her on the couch. Mrs. Meyer brought a cold cloth and put it on her forehead.

"I don't think she's been eating properly," she said. "Where has she been staying, Scot?"

Scot shook his head. "I don't know. Hiding out, I guess."

Evangeline opened her dark eyes and tried to sit up.

"Just lie still for a while," Mrs. Meyer said, gently pushing her down. "I'll put you in with Dawn, Evangeline. You're going to stay with us until your stepfather returns. OK?"

The girl nodded. "OK," she said faintly.

Jodi turned to go to Scot's room where she and Mary-Ann were sleeping. She frowned as she got out her pajamas. *How dramatic to faint and have Scot carry her around! If she hasn't been eating right, that's her fault!* she thought. She sat down on the edge of the bed, suddenly feeling guilty. It was clear that the girl really needed help. What was her part in this mystery?

A heavy, tight feeling of dread and fear pressed upon her. She sighed and crawled into bed. What was going to happen? What could she do about it all?

The next morning Jodi glanced out the window at the gray sky and shivered. *Snow, Evangeline said! Well, it sure looks like it today!*

"It's a real pretty lake," Scot was saying enthusiastically to MaryAnn at the breakfast table when Jodi came in a few minutes later. "Let's ride up there today and see it!"

Evangeline kept her eyes on her plate as Jodi sat down beside her. Mrs. Meyer, dressed and looking better, set a plate of steaming hotcakes on the table. Brian, Jodi learned, was sick and still in bed.

MaryAnn was smiling at Scot. "Wherever you lead I'll follow," she said. "This is beautiful country. I wish I could live here."

Evangeline glowered at her. "You could take my place any time," she said.

"I'm sure your stepfather will come back soon," Mrs.

93

Meyer said, patting Evangeline on the shoulder. Jodi saw a look of intense hate distort her pretty face.

"I hope not!" she spit out.

After breakfast Jodi pulled on her boots, zipped up her jacket, and followed MaryAnn outside. She sensed that Scot was trying to get them away from the house, away from this mystery that was so frightening and upsetting.

Up ahead, Scot yelled something. Jodi raised her head.

"The horses!" Scot was shouting. "They're gone!" He ran down the hill with Jodi, Evangeline, MaryAnn, and Dawn close on his heels. It was true! The gate was open and the horses were gone!

Jodi strode into the corral and stared around, her heart pounding. Over by the open gate, something was on the ground. She picked it up. *A broken feather!*

"It's the broken feather again," she called to Scot. He stepped over to her and took it from her fingers.

Suddenly Evangeline snatched it away from him and threw it down with a violent gesture.

"Go look for the horses!" she screamed, her dark eyes flashing. "Standing around staring at a stupid feather!"

Jodi stared at her, speechless. Evangeline's face was as pale as it had been last night, but now her eyes were blazing with anger. For once, it was MaryAnn who spoke first.

"It only stands to reason," she said, pushing her dark hair back, "that we should try to find out who let the horses loose."

Evangeline whirled and stomped out of the corral, her head bent low to study the road for tracks.

Scot followed her, and Jodi and MaryAnn came behind him. They studied the road, but there were horse tracks everywhere. Finally Scot looked up.

"Dawn, you and MaryAnn go back to the house and tell Mom what happened. Have her drive you up and down the main road, OK?" He glanced around. "Where's Evangeline?"

They looked, but she had disappeared. He shrugged.

"Oh, well. Jodi, let's you and I go up the trail and look around in the meadows." Jodi nodded, and they each picked up a bridle and started out. They passed the small lake where she had caught her breath the day before. It was ruffled now with a breeze.

Jodi shivered. "Scot, who's behind all this?" she asked.

"You know as well as I do," Scot answered. "It's got to be LaMoure. But why! That's what's got me stumped."

"But what about the broken feather, and the curse, Scot!" she said. "There's someone else involved, too. I know it! Someone on the reserve who's turning the Indians away from you!"

Scot nodded. "I know there is. But who? And again—why? Are they working together? I wouldn't be surprised if old Hercules is in on it, too."

They passed the cabin, but the old man did not come out.

She shook her head. "No, I think he's on the level. I came up here yesterday—" she paused when he shot her a disapproving look. "I was OK, honest! He's really friendly, if you give him time and show him you're interested in him. He doesn't smoke Camels, by the way. He makes his own."

He smiled at her, and the warmth in his smile thawed

out some of the tight knot of jealousy in her heart.

"You're OK, Jodi," he said softly. They emerged from the woods into a large open meadow.

"This is where we were the other day, isn't it?" Jodi said. "When the plane landed."

Scot nodded. "Dick Meadow. There's fresh tracks all over. Let's look around."

They moved further into the meadow. Suddenly Jodi saw something moving at the far end.

"There's some horses!" she exclaimed. "Do you think that's them?"

Scot started toward them. Jodi was about to follow when something caught her eye in the woods to her left. It had been a movement. She studied the woods. Was someone spying on them? Was it Evangeline? She heard some twigs snap, and then someone stepped out.

Charlie! She waited until he came closer. Scot paused and glanced back, then came running when he saw Charlie.

"What are you doing out here?" he asked the young Indian man.

Charlie frowned. "Looking for my horse. You know that black one? Someone let him loose last night from the reserve corral. I thought maybe he'd be up here in the meadows."

Scot nodded. "Someone let our horses loose, too. I think we've found them, though. Over there." He motioned to the group of horses at the far end of the meadow. "Your horse might be with them. Come on."

They jogged across the meadow and then slowed as they approached the horses. Jodi let out a long breath.

There were Paint, Red, and Buckskin. Scot called to them, and they raised their heads and shifted their feet. Scot walked slowly up to Paint and bridled him while Jodi slipped the bridle over Red's head. She put her foot in Scot's cupped hands and jumped up.

Scot leaped up on Paint. "Buckskin will follow behind," he said. "We'll ride on up, Charlie, and see if we can spot your horse." Charlie nodded, his eyes on the ground.

"Charlie caught that horse wild," Scot explained to Jodi as they trotted on up the trail. "He's real fond of it. I hope nothing's happened to it!"

Jodi nodded. She hoped so, too, but inside a terrible feeling of fear twisted her stomach into a knot. She glanced at Scot, and his face, too, was solemn.

They were following a creek through the woods, and then the woods opened up on a tiny meadow. Jodi pulled up on Red and gazed around. Several large, black crows were settling on something on the ground.

Scot rode Paint closer and then dismounted. The knot in Jodi's stomach tightened as the crows flapped away from the heap on the ground. It was black! She got off and walked over to Scot. He was standing in stunned silence, staring at a black horse lying not far away. Jodi's blue eyes widened.

The horse lay perfectly still, its head twisted back in an unnatural position. Flies buzzed around it.

"Oh, Scot! It's dead!" Tears stung her eyes, and her head swam. She turned to run away, but her knees buckled underneath her. Scot whirled and caught her up close.

She closed her eyes as the tears streamed down her face. She felt the roughness of his coat against her cheek and his strong arms. Her breath came in great sobs that tore at her throat.

Finally the sobs subsided and she pushed away from him. Walking to the stream, she sat down beside it on a large rock, her back to the dead horse. For a long while she sat looking at the twinkling water as it splashed over rocks and carried sticks along. She felt she was a stick, being swept along on a current of evil.

"Well, I found the bullet," Scot said, kneeling beside her. "And this." He held up a crumpled note with shaking fingers. Jodi read it silently.

This is what we do to traitors, white man! She gasped and looked into Scot's troubled blue eyes.

"Somebody did this on purpose!" she said, shaking her head.

He nodded. "I'm afraid so. Do you feel like riding yet?"

She went to Red. "The sooner I get out of here, the better!" He helped her up on Red and then mounted Paint. They rode back through the woods.

Jodi felt sick to her stomach. "Who would do that, Scot?"

"I don't know," he said, shaking his head. "It almost seems like an Indian person because of the reference to *traitor* in the note. But I don't think they would do it." He lapsed into silence. Around the next bend, Charlie approached them.

"We found your horse," Scot said in a low voice.

Charlie glanced up. "Where?" he asked eagerly, hope

springing into his eyes. But one look at Scot's pale, drawn face caused him to look down.

"Up in the meadow," Scot replied, and then very gently, "they only used one bullet. So he died fast. I'm— sorry." His voice broke and he looked away. Tears began flowing down Jodi's cheeks once more.

Charlie nodded slowly. He took off his cowboy hat and wiped his forehead. His face was grim.

"Charlie!" Jodi cried out. "Who did it? Do you know?"

He glanced up at her, anger flashing from his dark eyes.

"Yes, I know who did it!"

Back to the Shed

The young Indian man's face had paled, and his shoulders drooped. There was a long silence as Jodi waited with bated breath for the name of the person who shot his horse.

"Well, Charlie?" she asked finally, pulling up on Red's head. "Do you know who did it? We should tell the police!"

He stiffened suddenly, replaced his hat, and started out toward the meadow. They watched him disappear, and then turned to go home.

"I blew that one," Jodi said disgustedly. "I shouldn't have mentioned the police!"

Scot shook his head. "I don't think he would have told us, anyway."

The wind had picked up, and it was cold. Jodi shivered inside her jacket as she watched the gray clouds scudding across the sky and black ones forming on the horizon. What a night it was going to be!

Mrs. Meyer was setting the table for lunch when they came in. The radio was on, and MaryAnn and Dawn were peeling and slicing carrots.

"Well, we found them," Scot said.

MaryAnn glanced at him. "We saw you come in. You don't look very happy about it."

He took off his cowboy hat and hung it on a hook in the kitchen. Then he sat down to wrench off his boots.

100

"Our horses were OK," he said slowly. "Charlie's wasn't so lucky." Jodi excused herself and went to the bathroom. She could not bear to talk about it. She washed her face and hands and brushed her reddish brown hair.

"To Billy Tom at Redstone," the announcer on the radio read monotonously as Jodi stepped into the kitchen, "coming home today. Please pick me up. Signed, Linda."

Jodi sat down at the table, listening. "To John Meyer, please come home immediately. Signed, Becky. To Al Brown at Chezacut, we will meet—" Mrs. Meyer switched off the radio and sat down with a sigh.

"The only thing I don't like about that," she said after they had said the blessing, "is that the whole country listens in."

Scot nodded. "I don't like it, either. Let's just hope Dad gets home safely." Jodi glanced at him, and for a second she could see the fear in his eyes.

The porch door slammed shut, and Evangeline came into the room. She avoided looking at anyone and went straight to the bathroom. A few minutes later, she sat at the table.

"Did you find Thunder?" Scot asked her.

She nodded but did not look up. Her face was dark and troubled.

Jodi looked at the food and suddenly pushed herself away from the table.

"I'm really not hungry," she said to Mrs. Meyer. Listlessly she wandered out into the living room. Gazing out the windows she saw the dead horse once more in her

101

mind's eye. Who would do something that cruel?

The sky was dark now, and she heard the low moan of the wind in the trees. Once again she thought of the bizarre chain of events that led up to this moment. The prowler at the cabin, the unfriendliness of the Indian people, the planeload of boxes that turned out to be guns and who knew what else, Charlie and Marie's wrecked house, the trail of broken feathers left at each event, the curse of the wolf, and now someone shooting Charlie's horse. She rubbed her forehead.

One thing was clear—someone was masterminding a plot to drive the missionaries from the area! Was La-Moure behind it all? She shook her head. Maybe some fresh air would help.

"Going for a walk," she mumbled as she went through the kitchen and slung on her jacket. Outside she looked up at the storm that was coming and shivered. The wind tugged at her hair and pressed against her legs as she walked down to the corral.

Thunder lifted his head and whinnied. Jodi patted him for a moment, and then she heard the kitchen door slam. Maybe it was Evangeline, coming to ride Thunder. An idea sprang into her mind. She left the corral fence and opened the door of the small shed, slipping inside and closing the door silently.

Through a crack in the door she watched Evangeline approach. The slim girl peered through the corral fence and called softly to her horse. He came to her and nuzzled her hands. Suddenly she straightened, absolutely still, and studied the hillside and woods above her. Then she looked up toward the house, and then at the shed.

Jodi tensed. Had the Indian girl sensed someone spying on her?

Evangeline was listening, her head cocked to one side, her eyes on the woods. And then Jodi heard a low whistle. Suddenly, like a frightened deer, Evangeline darted around the corral and disappeared into the woods. Jodi opened the door of the shed, her heart pounding. Was she going to meet someone?

Quickly she sprinted up the hill and entered the woods, heading in the direction she had seen Evangeline take. Then up ahead she caught a flash of movement. *Evangeline!* Breathless, she slowed her steps and studied the ground, trying not to step on twigs or rustle the bushes. Silently she glided on, catching a glimpse of the girl now and then ahead of her.

Soon she saw Evangeline clearly. Through the bushes she could see her stop and look around. Jodi realized where she was now—at the bluff where she and Dawn and MaryAnn had seen Hercules that first night. A man came into view and began talking to Evangeline. Jodi caught her breath.

Leech!

She had to hear what they were saying! Carefully she picked her way through the bushes, edging closer.

Evangeline and her stepfather seemed to be having an argument.

"I won't do it, I tell you!" Evangeline said loudly, stamping her foot.

Leech shrugged. "Don't make no difference, really, kid," he said amiably. "We'll get 'em out one way or another. I hear Scot's dad is coming home. You know I

103

could do the same to him as I did to that horse of Charlie's!" He smiled slowly, his eyes gleaming with hate. He lit a cigarette and puffed on it.

Evangeline whirled on him. "You wouldn't!" she screamed. "You're a dirty coward!" He slapped her hard, and she stumbed back, holding her face.

Now he was angry. "You'll tell us when Scot's father gets home, ya hear? Maybe I wouldn't do nothing, but here's a fellar who would!" Stamping out his cigarette on the ground, he put his finger to his lips and whistled.

Another man emerged from the bushes and stood beside Leech on the bluff. He seemed oddly out of place, wearing a dark suit, a felt hat pulled low over his eyes, and dark glasses. A chill coursed through Jodi's body. *Who is this? A gangster?*

His voice was oily as he approached Evangeline.

"Listen, kid," he said softly, "we'll make it worth your while. I'm ready to give you two hundred bucks right now, and two hundred more when you give us the information we want. Look." He put his hand in a suit pocket and pulled out a handful of money.

Evangeline backed away from him, not even glancing at the money. She was staring at Leech. Jodi was sure she had never seen such hate and loathing on anyone's face before. It twisted her pretty face until it was ugly.

"Leave me alone, Leech," she said slowly, "I'm not your daughter. I never want to see you again!" With that she leaped toward him and with a sudden push sent him flying over the edge of the bluff.

"Why, you—" the man with the black hat exclaimed, grabbing her arms. She hit him hard in the stomach with her elbow, squirmed out of his hands, and disappeared into the woods.

He started to follow her, but then turned back to the cliff. Jodi could hear Leech moaning from down below. The man leaped over the bluff and disappeared. She could hear them talking, and then their voices faded away.

She was alone. She hugged herself and paced back and forth in a small clearing nearby. What did it all mean? Oh, if she could only figure it out.

First of all, Leech was in on it somehow. Or was he behind it all? Being on the reserve, he could turn the Indian people against the missionary. And he was the one who shot Charlie's horse! Evangeline, had been spying on them and giving the information to her step-father.

Burning anger filled her mind. *That little sneak!* After all the Meyers had done for her, she was betraying them behind their backs. Well, she would put an end to that! She imagined how she would confront Evangeline in front of Scot. Oh, how she would make her squirm. And then they would call the police, and—

She stopped. What had the Bible said? To love your enemies and forgive those who do you wrong? She pushed the thought aside and stepped out onto the bluff.

Leech had had a cigarette. Where did he drop it? She searched for a few minutes and then found the half-smoked cigarette. Gingerly she picked it up. Yes, it was a Camel.

She pocketed it and turned back into the woods at a trot. Now she had enough proof. She would call the police, and they would have to come out and arrest Leech.

At the house, she noticed the van was gone. Had Mrs. Meyer gone somewhere? She glanced down at the corral. Thunder was gone. Where had Evangeline gone? Somehow she felt disappointed that her moment of putting the squeeze on the girl would have to wait.

She dashed into the house. The kitchen was empty and silent. There was a light on in the living room, so she went in there. Brian lay on the couch reading comics. He glanced up when she came in.

"Where have you been?" he asked. "Evangeline came in and said that Mr. Meyer was in danger! Mrs. Meyer and the others went in the van to meet him and warn him."

Jodi paced up and then down the living room. "I overheard Evangeline and Leech talking, Brian. There's something big going on. Evangeline had been spying on us, but now she's turned. I think she's really frightened." She paused and turned to him.

"Brian, we've got to call the police!" she exclaimed, her eyes wide. "Leech is the one who was prowling around the cabin! Look! I found this Camel cigarette and he dropped it!" She held out the squashed half-smoked cigarette. "And I heard him say he shot Charlie's horse!"

He sat up and shook his head. "Mrs. Meyer already called!" he said. "They said they couldn't come tonight. They need more proof. They said they'd come first thing Monday morning to investigate."

"Investigate!" Jodi exploded. "What are we going to do in the meantime? Just let them clobber us all?"

"I don't know." Brian sighed and sank back on the couch.

She paced back and forth, her mind working on the problem. If only she could get more proof! But how? And where? Suddenly she thought of the shed behind LaMoure's cabin. Would that bear searching again?

"Well, I gotta go," she said.

"Where!" he demanded.

She whirled down the hall. "Just out!" she called back. Dashing into Scot's room she picked up a small flashlight from his desk and then looked at the two-way radios. Should she take one of them? Finally she picked one up and then wrote a note and placed it on the other radio.

"Turn this on," the note read. She ran back down the hall and stopped at the living room. "Tell Scot to go in his room when he gets back," she said to Brian. "I may need him."

Brian called after her, but she ran to the door and flew down the hill to the corral. Something cold was stinging her face. *Snow!* So Evangeline's prophecy had come true. She bridled and saddled Red, opened the corral gate, and sprang into the saddle.

Like a shot, Red thundered up the hill and flew down the road. *Well, at least he is ready to go!* she thought. *Reddy! Hey, that's his name!* As she clung to the saddle, his long mane slapping her face, and the cold wind biting through her jacket, her mind raced ahead. Just what did she expect to find? How was she going to get into the shed? What if the dogs barked?

Around the next corner she spotted the faint trail leading into the woods. She slowed her horse and turned him off the road. The back of LaMoure's cabin came into view, and she dismounted, tied Red to a tree, and crept up to the small shed.

Her heart was pounding as she peered around the corner. A big black car was parked in the driveway next to several pickups. *Looks like the whole gang is here,* she thought. *Boy, I sure hope I don't get caught!*

For several minutes her resolve wavered as she crouched in the semidarkness behind the shed. The wind was howling now, and the snow was falling in hard, sharp pellets. She waited until the hailstorm was over and the snow was drifting down silently from the black sky.

Then, very carefully, she raised herself and explored around the outside of the shed. She could not use the door, and it would be locked, anyway. On the side near the woods, she found a small window and her spirits lifted.

Would it open? She pushed on it tentatively, but it was so rusty it would not budge. She struggled with it for some time and then found a rock and a stick. Placing the rock beside the bottom of the window, she pried upward with the stick. The stick snapped. She paused, waiting to see if the dogs would begin barking.

All was quiet. She got a stronger piece of two-by-four and pried against the window with that. This time the window popped. She pried up against it several times, and she could see the window move a little each time. Now she tried to open it. It moved! She glanced around and saw a chunk of wood. Dragging it to the window, she climbed up on it and with better leverage pushed against the window again. This time it screeched and opened.

She listened. Had anyone heard that? There was no sounds from the cabin, or footsteps approaching. Very slowly she eased herself through the window and into the dark shed.

She was sitting on a box. Turning on her flashlight, she beamed it around the small, cluttered shed. She leaped up and began opening boxes.

She lifted a bottle out of one box. It was liquor. *So LaMoure runs a little bootlegging business on the side! Well, he could be arrested for that!* She straightened and flashed the light around again. She had to find something else, something that would prove—

Her light illumined a large black briefcase. Somehow it seemed out of place in the shambles of the shed. She went to it and opened it. It was filled with money! There were neat stacks of fives, tens, and twenties bound together with strips of white paper. She touched the money to make sure it was real. Somehow she felt like she was playing Monopoly.

Inside one of the pockets in the lid she found a book, and she recognized it as some kind of ledger. She opened it. There was a piece of paper stapled to the inside of the front cover. Her eyes scanned it.

"Bernie Tom," she read out loud. "Be careful. He is suspicious. Charlie Henry. Give him all the booze he wants. He'll never know what you pay him." She glanced on down a long list, realizing that these were Indian men who worked for LaMoure in the mill. Beside each name was inside information concerning that man.

She turned the page. The next contained records of the payroll at the mill. But someone had tampered with the amounts to be paid to the men. Where one was supposed to be paid $250, that amount would be changed to read $200. On and on she read, flipping the pages.

Suddenly she realized where all the money in the briefcase had come from. *LaMoure is cheating the Indian men out of their paychecks!* And someone on the reserve was supplying him with information on how best to do it. That would be Leech, of course.

She snapped the briefcase shut and picked up the ledger. This was all she would need to prove what LaMoure was up to. She stood up, and then froze. Men's voices! They were coming toward the shed!

8

The Chapel First

Jodi glanced around frantically. Where could she hide? Suddenly she saw a small space behind some boxes in the corner. She dived toward the opening, squeezed herself in, and pulled a gunnysack over her feet.

There was the sound of a key in the lock. *The window!* She had not closed it. But it was too late now. The door opened and she heard men's voices as they stepped into the shed.

"Look at that window!" A man's voice growled. "Someone's been in here!" *That was Leech!* "Those snoopy kids. Well, they won't get far." He chuckled deep in his throat, and Jodi swallowed hard, hoping they couldn't hear her heart pounding.

There was the sound of boxes being moved, and she froze with fear. Would they discover her hiding place? Several other men came in, and there was the sound of a box lid being pried off.

"Here, fellas," Leech said. "Take your pick. Aren't they beauties?" From the conversation that followed, she realized they were looking at guns. A sweat formed on her forehead, and prickly goosebumps covered her arms.

The men began to leave, and she heard Leech's growling laugh boom out.

"Big game hunting tonight, boys!" he said, shutting the door and locking it. She heard steps and voices going away.

She crawled out from behind the boxes, her knees shaking and her head swimming. What did Leech mean by big game hunting tonight? Was that other man a hired gun? Were they going to shoot the missionaries?

For a moment panic seized her. She scrambled out of the window, clutching the ledger under her arm. She wanted to run, to get as far away from those men as possible! She wanted to go home. She dropped down in the snow and glanced around. Large fluffy snowflakes were drifting down, and the silence of the woods calmed her mind.

Suddenly she remembered the radio in her pocket. Getting it out, she turned it on.

"Jodi to Scot," she said into the mouthpiece. "Come in, please!" *Oh, Lord, please help him to answer!* she thought. She repeated the message, but there was no reply. She pocketed the radio and glanced toward the cabin.

Should she go and get help? But then she realized it would be too late by the time the police got here. *Too late!*

"Oh!" She covered her face with her shaking hands as she gave in to the despair that flooded over her. Sobs shook her body as she thought of what those awful men were planning to do. But then it seemed as if a gentle hand was placed on her shoulder, and peace filled her heart. She lifted her wet face.

"Thank you, Lord," she whispered into the darkness. "Help me know what to do now, and keep Mr. Meyer safe."

Holding the ledger tightly, she edged down the side of

the shed until she could see the cabin with its bright lights, the front yard, and the pickups parked not far away. She still had no plan of action, but one thing was clear—she had to warn Mr. Meyer before he got home! How could she do that?

She looked at the pickup that was parked closest to the shed. Leaning over, she ran up to it. Maybe she could drain out the gas, or do something to the motor. But there were too many vehicles here! She would have to fix every one, and there was no time!

The cabin door opened, and light streamed out into the yard. Jodi ducked down behind the pickup, her heart thudding heavily. They were on their way to do whatever crime they had planned! How could she stop them?

She glanced into the bed of the truck. Hey! There was a large wooden storage box in the back. Maybe if she went along—not thinking any further, she leaped into the bed of the truck, opened the lid of the box, and dropped inside. It was stuffy and smelled strongly of gas. Voices approached. Several men got in the cab, slammed the doors, and the motor roared to life.

Bouncing out the driveway and down the road, Jodi clenched her fists so tight her fingernails dug into her palms. After a while, she opened the lid of the box a fraction of an inch and peered out. They were heading for the mission station! As they neared the property, the men slowed down and turned off the lights!

At the road leading to the small cabin, the truck slowed and a door opened. Someone jumped out.

"You'll only get one shot," Leech called from inside

113

the cab. The man muttered something, the door shut, and they went on.

"Oh, Lord, keep Mr. Meyer safe," Jodi whispered. Then the truck stopped and the motor was shut off. The other men got out. Jodi lifted the lid a tiny bit. They were at the chapel! LaMoure was standing near the truck, speaking in a low voice to Leech.

"We'll burn this first," he said. "Come on, let's case the joint and then get the gas." They stepped toward the chapel and quietly opened the door. Jodi felt a can by her feet. The gas can! She had to get out. Quickly she lifted the lid and climbed out, dropping down on the far side of the truck. What should she do now? Go for help?

But just then one of the men returned, reached into the box in the truck, and took out the gas can. Jodi saw by the dim light of his flashlight that it was LaMoure. He took the can into the chapel.

Jodi was frantic. If she did not do something quick, the chapel would go up in flames! Suddenly she remembered the radio in her pocket. Oh, if only Scot had his on! She took it out and turned it on. Pushing the "talk" button, she called for Scot. There was nothing. She tried again, and then again. Nothing. She looked at the chapel and could see a flash of light.

Desperate now, she crept up the steps and into the chapel. She could hear low voices in the one large room inside. Laying the ledger she had carried down on a bench, she inched her way into the room. When she reached the center aisle, she could see two men crouched over something about halfway up the aisle. She could see the faint glow of their flashlights.

114

Slowly she crept closer, feeling each board before she put her full weight on it. *Two against one,* she thought. *My only hope is surprise, and then to get away. That may delay them enough to get help.*

The men straightened their legs. She crouched down not three feet away. LaMoure reached into his pocket for a match. It was now or never.

With a blood-curdling scream, she leaped at Leech and knocked him flying. He crashed into LaMoure, and they both tumbled to the floor. Jodi grabbed for the pile of gas-soaked papers, but LaMoure regained his feet and grabbed her arm. She whirled around and sank her teeth into his hand. With a howl he let loose. She turned to run, but precious seconds had been lost, and now Leech lunged for her.

He grabbed her arm and twisted it behind her back. Quick as a cat, she broke his hold and took several more leaps toward the door. *Almost there!* Then LaMoure had her again. It was a strong body hold, her arms pinned tightly against her sides. Leech came up.

"Wildcat!" LaMoure panted. Jodi's first impulse was to struggle, but she resisted it, remembering her training. *Submit! Pretend to be defeated, but watch for that one unguarded moment.*

"What are we going to do with her?" Leech asked gruffly.

LaMoure kept his grip tight on her arms and walked her out the door and toward the truck.

"Take her back to the cabin, and tie her up," he said. "We'll hold her as a hostage until we get what we want. You get in and drive. I'll hold her in the back here."

Stepping up on the tailgate, he hefted her up into the truck.

If only she could get a message to Scot. Desperately she wiggled one hand until it reached her pocket. She pushed it in and felt the radio. Turning it on, she pushed the talk button.

The truck started with a lurch, and she lost the button for a few seconds. There, she had it again! Now what was SOS? Then she remembered. She pushed the button down—three longs, three shorts, three longs.

She withdrew her hand, and suddenly her body tensed. The truck had slowed down to make a turn, and La-Moure leaned over to say something to Leech. Jodi knew her moment had come. With one swift twist of her body, she broke his hold and leaped away from his grasp. He gave a cry of surprise and lunged for her. But without hesitation, she jumped over the side of the truck.

She hit the road hard on her hands and knees, and then rolled down the embankment. Pain rocketed up through her knees, and she heard shouting in the distance, and the gravel flying as the truck screeched to a stop. She had to get to her feet!

Her head spinning, she stumbled to her feet. Two flashlights bobbed down the road toward her—was it Leech and LaMoure? She tried to turn and run to the woods, but suddenly she was sinking in blackness. And the shouts grew closer!

9

Learning to Love

"Let me go!" Jodi screamed, fighting against the hands that held her. And then she heard a voice just above her head. Her eyes flew open. *Scot!* Her head was resting on his jacket, and someone was leaning over.

"Jodi! Are you OK?" It was Mr. Meyer!

She smiled at Scot's tall, handsome father. "I—I guess so," she said. "Thank goodness you're all right!" She sat up and looked around. "What happened to LaMoure and Leech?"

"I don't know for sure," Mr. Meyer said, straightening up. "The police were chasing them down the road. I was just behind the police cars. What's going on, anyway?"

Scot took her hand and helped her to her feet.

"Lots, Dad!" he said. "We'll tell you all about it when we get home. Mom and I went down the road to meet you and warn you because your life had been threatened. But when you didn't come, we decided to pray about it and leave it with the Lord. When we got home, I saw the note Jodi left on the two-way radio and I was worried. So I started out for LaMoure's cabin. Then I heard the SOS she sent, and saw her jump from the truck."

Just then a police car stopped on the road nearby. Mr. Meyer strode over to it, and, with Scot's help, Jodi hobbled up.

"Did you catch them?" she asked the officer.

117

He nodded. "Yeah, we got Leech and LaMoure. But we're going to have to let them go if we can't find something to pin on them."

"There's lots to pin on them!" Jodi exclaimed. "I found boxes of booze in the shed behind LaMoure's cabin, and guns, and a briefcase full of money! LaMoure's been cheating the Indian men out of their paychecks! I found a ledger that proves it all! And there's another guy around here somewhere who's got a gun, and they were saying they were going to shoot Mr. Meyer!"

"Where is the ledger now?" the police officer asked.

"In the back of the chapel, sir," Jodi replied. She pointed out the small building behind the trees. "On one of the benches. Leech and LaMoure were going to burn the chapel! I saw them! Then they caught me and were going to hold me as a hostage. But I got away."

The officer nodded, picking up his radio. "That all figures. We've known something was going on out here for some time." He spoke into the radio and then drove off toward the chapel.

Mr. Meyer and Scot helped Jodi to their pickup, which was parked at the side of the road not too far away.

"Oh!" Jodi exclaimed suddenly. "I left Reddy behind the shed at LaMoure's, Mr. Meyer."

Scot looked at her. "Reddy?"

She laughed. "Yup. I named Red Reddy, Scot. Because he's always ready to go, and I sure appreciated that this afternoon!"

Mr. Meyer grinned. "OK, Reddy it is. I'll drive down there, and Scot can ride him home."

A few minutes later they pulled into LaMoure's driveway. A police car pulled in behind them, and two officers jumped out. Jodi pointed out the shed, and they headed toward it.

"It's locked," Jodi remarked as Scot got out. "The window on the far side opens, Scot. Show them that." He nodded and waved.

Mr. Meyer turned the pickup around. "Quite a night, Jodi. I'm still pretty much in the dark about what's going on."

At the Meyers' house she opened the door of the pickup and stepped out, but pain shot up from her knees and she crumpled to the ground. Mr. Meyer dashed around to help her.

"Here," he said, picking her up, "you're not such a load." He carried her into the house.

"One victim here," he announced as he came in. Mrs. Meyer rose from the table and rushed over to Jodi. MaryAnn and Dawn were close behind her.

"What happened, Jodi?" Mrs. Meyer asked. "Bring her to Scot's room, John. Oh, my! I'm glad you're home and safe!" She gave him a quick hug and wiped tears from her eyes.

"And Jodi, too," Dawn said earnestly. "We've just been praying for you, Jodi. What happened?"

Jodi grinned as Mr. Meyer laid her gently on Scot's bed, but then she grew serious once more.

"Leech and LaMoure were going to burn down the chapel," she said as Mrs. Meyer examined her bloody hands and knees. "I didn't have time to go for help, so I tried to stop them. They grabbed me and were taking me back to LaMoure's cabin, when I got away and jumped out of their truck."

Mrs. Meyer left the room to get some first aid supplies. Jodi winced when she cleansed the wounds and dressed them. She was glad when it was all over.

"Now you need some supper," Mrs. Meyer told her. "Here, lean on Dawn and me and we'll help you out."

It was a busy night in the Meyers' kitchen. Mrs. Meyer had just finished heating Jodi's supper when there was a loud banging on the door. It was Charlie. He came in, sat down at the table with everyone else, and accepted a mug of hot coffee. Everyone was talking at once, filling Mr. Meyer in on the trouble they had been having.

Jodi finished her supper, hardly hearing the conversation around her. Where was Evangeline? Had the police found the ledger? Would they arrest Leech and LaMoure? And had they found that gangster?

There was a commotion just outside the door and Jodi recognized Scot's voice. Mr. Meyer went to the door and opened it. Evangeline, disheveled and angry, stood just outside the door. Scot was behind her, and he pushed her in. He was holding her arm very firmly.

"You're coming in whether you want to or not," Scot said, steering her toward a chair.

"What's this all about, son?" Mr. Meyer asked.

Scot shook his head, gazing at the Indian girl who sat with her shoulders slumped and her head down.

"She hasn't had anything to eat for dinner," he told his father. "I found her sleeping in the shed by the corral just now. She doesn't have anyone to live with now, and Mom said she is to stay here. So I brought her up, and had to fight her every step of the way."

Mrs. Meyer began cooking another supper. Jodi glanced at Evangeline and smiled. So the spy was caught! Maybe now she could tell Scot what she had overheard on the bluff, and he would see her for the rotten person she was. She opened her mouth to begin, but once more there was knocking on the front door.

Mr. Meyer strode over to the door and let in two police officers. One of them carried the ledger. Evangeline shrank back as they sat down at the table near her, and her hair hid her face completely.

"Well, we got Leech and LaMoure and the other fellow who was here," the dark-haired officer began. "By the way, he was a hired gun from Vancouver that LaMoure brought in."

He drew out a pad and pen from his pocket. "Now we just need a statement from you folks and we'll be on our way."

Mr. Meyer rubbed his chin thoughtfully. "From what I gather, LaMoure was behind a scheme to drive us out of the area. He was also trying to turn the Indian people away from us. But why? That's what I don't understand."

The police officer leaned back. "LaMoure had quite a racket going here," he said, picking up the ledger. "Swindling money from the Indians, bootlegging booze, storing stolen goods from gangs in the Vancouver area. You see, LaMoure is just an alias. When we checked some mug shots in Williams Lake, we realized he's wanted in several provinces." He set the ledger down and accepted some coffee from Mrs. Meyer.

"He had a little help, too," the other officer went on. "Leech was in on it, but we don't have much on him yet."

"He tried to burn down the chapel!" Jodi nearly yelled, angry that Leech might get off lightly. "I saw that! And he was helping LaMoure by supplying him with information about the Indian people. He was the one who was prowling around the cabin! I have proof of that!"

She glanced around, and everyone was staring at her.

"We picked up the butt of a Camel cigarette outside the cabin," she said smugly. "And I saw Leech drop one when he and Evangeline were talking on the bluff this afternoon." She saw the girl stiffen, and she hurried on. "Leech was the one who was trying to drive you out! He and LaMoure were afraid you would find out what they were doing! And Evangeline was their spy! She told Leech we were staying in the cabin that night, and all sorts of things. She—"

Scot squeezed her arm. "That's enough, Jodi," he said.

She pulled away and turned back to the officers. "And Leech is the one who shot Charlie's—"

"Jodi!" Charlie broke in, standing up. His face was red. "I don't want anyone to know!"

"But—but, *Charlie!* He should be punished!" Jodi replied, her face burning and her mind whirling.

He stood up to his full height and reached for his cowboy hat. "No!" he said firmly. "I, too, should be punished! God forgave me, and I should do the same to Leech. No, I don't want him punished. I forgive him in my heart. I love him, and pray for him. My horse is gone. Who can bring him back?" He turned and walked quietly out of the house.

Jodi sank back in her chair, tears springing to her eyes. She saw Evangeline had not touched her food, but sat with her face in her hands. Scot had stepped over to her and was saying something to her quietly.

Suddenly she felt miserable. Evangeline deserved to be told on of course, but had it really been necessary? Had it really helped her? She struggled to her feet, unable to hold back the tears any longer. Dawn sprang to her side, and she began limping from the room.

"We don't want to press charges, either," Mr. Meyer was saying quietly. "We just want the harrassment to stop."

The officer stood up, and Jodi glanced back. "It'll stop, all right," he said firmly. "We have enough on them to put them up for a while. Good night."

Jodi shuffled on to the bedroom, thanked Dawn, and shut the door. She hobbled over to the bed and sank down on it, sobbing into her hands. *Oh, how wrong I have been! How mean and cruel!* She remembered Charlie's words. *But God forgave me, and I should do the same to him. I forgive him in my heart. I love him, and pray for him.* She shook her head. *There's Charlie— a new Christian and yet he has such courage and forgiveness.*

Suddenly she hated the black jealousy in her heart that kept her from loving and forgiving.

"Oh, Lord," she sobbed, "I'm so ashamed of the way I've been feeling and acting! You've shown me tonight how to love. God, I know that I've sinned against you and others. Forgive my sin, and wash me clean by the blood of Jesus. Help me to forgive Evangeline, and—and Mona, too." She sighed and looked up. "Thank you, Lord."

She reached for a Kleenex, feeling better inside. But she knew she had something to do.

"MaryAnn!" she called at the top of her voice. Soon the dark-haired girl appeared at the door.

"Could you tell, I mean *ask* Evangeline to come here for a minute?" she asked.

MaryAnn shook her head. "She left, Jodi. Soon after the police left, she ran out. Scot went after her, but he hasn't come back, either."

Jodi stood up, clenching her teeth. "She's probably down at the corral. I have to go down there, MaryAnn. I just have to! Could you get me my jacket? I'll slip out the back door."

MaryAnn returned a few minutes later and handed her the jacket.

"Can I help?" she asked as Jodi hobbled out of the room. Jodi shook her head.

"No, this is one thing I have to do myself. I kind of like the pain. I guess I sort of deserve it."

Outside, she stumbled along in the darkness. The snow had turned to rain, and underfoot it was slushy and slick. Slowly she picked her way down the hill. There was Scot! He would know where Evangeline was.

At the corral, she saw Evangeline in the corral, saddling Thunder. Scot was trying to get her to come back. He turned when he heard her footsteps.

"Oh, it's you," he said. His voice was flat. Was he angry? Disappointed in her?

She blinked back the tears and looked at the Indian girl.

"Can I talk to you, Evangeline?" she said softly. But the girl continued to saddle her horse, never once acknowledging Jodi's presence. Scot walked back up the hill. Jodi slipped through the long fence and came closer to Evangeline.

"Evangeline," she said softly, "I know you must hate me, and I deserve every bit of it." Evangeline swung around and looked at Jodi for a second, but then she turned back. The saddling was done now, but she made no move to mount.

"I was wrong!" Jodi said earnestly. "I was wrong to be so bitter and jealous of you! I was jealous because Scot likes you a lot better than he likes me, and because you're so pretty." Evangeline whirled to face her again. Jodi continued. "I—I just want to say I'm sorry, and—and could we be friends?"

Tears began spilling out of the Indian girl's eyes.

"You—you mean you limped all the way down here to say you're *sorry?*" She asked, fighting against the tears. Jodi nodded, tears streaming down her cheeks.

"But I'm the one that was wrong, Jodi! I should be asking you to forgive me! I betrayed all of you! Anyway, Scot doesn't like me, and I'm *not* pretty! He just feels obligated. I'm an Indian, and he has to be nice to me!" Sobs shook her body, and she covered her face with her hands. Jodi threw her arm around her slim shoulders, suddenly seeing something she had never seen before— Evangeline's desperate need to be loved and appreciated.

"He *does* like you!" she heard herself saying. "I've

125

seen it in his eyes when he looks at you. It's not just duty, either, Evangeline. Scot isn't like that, and you know it. He really cares for you, and so do all the Meyers. They're waiting to help you. Are you going to let them?"

10

Power Failure

It did not take long to remove the saddle and bridle from one puzzled horse. Jodi, leading Evangeline by the hand, was dripping wet when she stepped into the kitchen.

Mr. and Mrs. Meyer were in the living room, but Scot, Dawn, MaryAnn, and Brian were sitting at the table. Scot hopped up when they came in.

"Here, sit down," he said to Evangeline. "I've kept your dinner warm. Want it now?"

Evangeline nodded, her large brown eyes shining and her dark hair plastered wet on her forehead. Jodi sank wearily down on a chair. Her knees were hurting, and she was tired. *Scot must hate me,* she thought sadly.

"Scot," Evangeline said in her low, musical voice. "All of you, really. I—I want to tell you something. First I want to say I'm sorry for spying on you for my stepfather. He said he'd shoot my horse if I didn't, and I knew he would. He hates all animals. I was so afraid! And I felt so alone. There was no one I could really talk to. And when you and your family were so nice to me it made me feel worse because I knew what a traitor I was!" she paused.

"Evangeline," Scot said, touching her arm. "You don't have to do this. We don't hold anything against you."

She shook her head. "But I want to, Scot! Please

listen. Bert had a hold on me, and I was scared. I guess you don't think very clearly when you're scared. I didn't think anyone really loved me. Bert was turning the Indian people against you guys. He told them he got a powerful witchdoctor from Alberta to put a strong curse on the reserve if anyone listened to you. It was the curse of the broken feather. And he used it, too, to make it look like the Indians were doing all the bad things around here."

Jodi nodded. "He was working the two sides against each other. Did you know he had just gone into hiding when you found that note?"

"At first I thought he had been kidnapped," Evangeline replied, "but then he got in touch with me. He was staying with LaMoure for a while, and then rented a cabin at the store. He paid the witchdoctor here to put a curse on you, too. He disappeared to cover his tracks so we wouldn't suspect him."

Scot leaned back. "Well, it's all over with, Evangeline. Let's just forget it!"

She shook her head. "I'm not finished. I said I didn't think anyone loved me, and certainly I didn't deserve to be loved. But Jodi helped show me tonight what real love is." Her voice choked off for a second and then she smiled at Jodi. "I'm beginning to understand the love of God that they're always talking about!"

Jodi squeezed her hand. "Then it's worth it all, Evangeline," she said softly.

The next morning Jodi sat on the edge of the bed, flexing her knees.

"Feel better?" MaryAnn asked, brushing her long, dark hair.

Jodi grimaced. "They don't hurt so bad, but they're sure sore! Guess I'll have to hobble today!" She stood up and dressed, folding her pajamas neatly into her suitcase. She sighed.

"We're going home today, and now that I'm friends with Evangeline, I'd like to stay and get better acquainted with her."

MaryAnn nodded. "I love it out here. Maybe I can talk Dad into buying a hunting cabin, and we could come more often." She shook her head. "Scot and Dawn are lucky."

"It's not luck." Jodi laughed. "But it would be nice to live here!"

After they had finished the daily Bible reading and prayer around the breakfast table, Mr. Meyer said that they would soon be leaving for Williams Lake, where Jodi, Brian, and MaryAnn would catch the bus for home. Jodi stood to help clean up the kitchen when the dogs began barking and someone knocked on the door. It was Charlie.

"Come in," Mr. Meyer said congenially. Mrs. Meyer poured him a cup of coffee and he flashed a smile, took off his cowboy hat, and sat down.

Finally the small talk died down and Charlie came to the reason for his visit.

"I was over at my grandfather's this morning," he said. He paused long enough to drain his coffee cup, and Jodi waited. She knew there was no use trying to hurry him. Mrs. Meyer leaned over to her.

"His grandfather," she whispered, "is Henry Jack, the witchdoctor!" Jodi stifled an exclamation and looked at Charlie.

"He said he wants to talk to you," Charlie said and stood up. "We go now."

Mr. Meyer stood and put on his cowboy hat. "Sure. Come along, honey."

She untied her apron and then looked at Jodi. "OK. I think it might be good for Jodi to go along, too. Is that all right?"

"Sure. Let's get going, though." He went outside to start the van.

"Can I come, too, Mom?" Scot asked. His mother nodded.

Jodi grabbed her jacket and limped out to the van. The sun was behind a cloud, but the air was crisp and clean after the night before. It smelled of fir and pine. Jodi took a deep breath. The only thing that bothered her was Scot. He had seemed nervous and had avoided her eyes. Was he still mad?

Soon they pulled up to the log cabin where Charlie's grandfather lived. The old man came out and welcomed them in. He was stooped, and his face was like a piece of wrinkled, weathered leather. They found seats on the bed along the wall, and Mr. Meyer and Henry Jack sat on the only two chairs in the one-room cabin.

Jodi gazed around. There was a big black wood stove in the center of the cabin with a big pot on it. Something was stewing in the pot. There was the rickety table, some wooden boxes that served as cabinets, and the bed in the back. Pegs in the wall held clothes and guns. An old kerosine lamp was on the table.

No one had been saying anything much at all for quite a while. Mr. Meyer had made a few comments about the weather and fishing, to which the old man nodded and grunted. Finally he pierced Mr. Meyer with his bright eyes.

"You tell me your God," he said gutterally. He turned to Charlie and uttered a long sentence in Chilcotin. Charlie then turned to Mr. Meyer.

"He says he wants to hear about your God because his spirits failed him. All his life he has been a witchdoctor. Always to help people, cure sickness, drive away bad spirits; never to hurt anyone. Until a white man tricked him to put big curse of the wolf on the missionary." He paused and gazed off into space.

"He says his spirits failed him. No more power. Now he wants to hear of your God. You'll tell me, I'll tell him."

Jodi sat with bated breath, her sparkly blue eyes wide, listening to Mr. Meyer tell the beautiful and simple gospel story to Charlie and then listening as Charlie turned to his grandfather to repeat it in Chilcotin. She watched as the old man's face lit up with the truth of God's love and grace.

Finally Mr. Meyer paused, fixing his eyes on the old man.

"Henry, do you want Jesus?" he asked. "You pray? Give your life to Him?"

The old man needed no interpreter to understand. He nodded firmly.

"Yes," he said. "I pray." His eyes squeezed shut, and as he prayed, Jodi felt tears trickling down her cheeks.

"Oh, great Jesus-God of this missionary, I pray you. Take away my badness. Clean my insides. I want you my God. I no longer pray to Indian spirits. Amen."

Jodi looked up. A bright ray of sun suddenly shone into the cabin through the one small window. The old man smiled. Mrs. Meyer, sitting nearby, squeezed her hand, and Jodi saw tears on her cheeks.

Mr. Meyer continued talking through Charlie to the old man. After a while, Henry got to his feet and brought out a box filled with fetishes, figures, feathers, and plants used in his craft. He walked with the box to the wood stove, opened the lid, and in one quick movement dumped the entire boxful into the stove.

"Praise the Lord!" Mrs. Meyer said quietly at her side. She reached over and gave Jodi a quick hug.

"Thanks for letting me come along," Jodi whispered to her, wiping the tears from her eyes.

Mrs. Meyer smiled. "I think this will prove to be the breakthrough we've been needing. Henry is very influential, and I know God is going to use him." She shook her head as they got ready to go. "I've never seen anyone turn so completely from the old religion and embrace Christ!"

Outside, Scot approached her before they got into the van.

"It's not far through the woods, Jodi," he said in a funny voice, "will you walk back with me?"

Jodi nodded. "If you don't walk too fast, I guess."

"Don't take too long, Scot," Mr. Meyer said when Scot told him. "We've got to get to town or these kids will miss that bus."

Scot nodded and turned to walk down the trail that led through the trees and over a small creek. Jodi trailed along beside him, wondering if he was going to bawl her out for acting so badly last night.

Finally, just before they crossed the plank that was a makeshift bridge over the creek, Scot paused and turned to her. She swallowed and braced herself.

"I want to tell you something," he said huskily. "I guess the right word is *confess*. I—I knew it was Leech for some time, Jodi."

She stared at him, too surprised to say anything for a minute.

"What do you mean?" she asked finally.

He looked down. "Well, after we found that cigarette butt by the cabin, I saw Evangeline with a pack of Camels. I asked her what she was doing with them, because I knew she didn't smoke. She got so flustered and guilty-looking that I guessed she was taking them to her father. And I knew he was the one prowling around the cabin. It was part of his plan to scare us all out of here, I guess." He paused, and they walked across the plank.

"Then that day you saw a movement up in the woods above the corral, I went up there first, and I saw him then. But I didn't say anything."

She frowned. "Why?"

"I didn't want to hurt Evangeline. I—I really didn't know anything for sure, and I thought that bringing it out would hurt her. I can see I was wrong now, but it's too

133

late. Anyway, I'm sorry, Jodi. It matters a lot to me that you understand and forgive me."

He stopped and gazed at her, and the look in his clear blue eyes made her heart stop. And then it began thumping loudly.

"Sure, I forgive you, Scot," she said, her face burning. She started to move on down the trail. "We'd better get going."

He walked beside her, chuckling softly, and took her hand. "It won't work, Jodi! You're always pushing me away! Well, I won't go away! I'm going to stick around liking you, whether you want me to or not!"

She smiled up at him. "Thanks, Scot."

Two things happened the next Friday that made it a very special day for Jodi. All week she had been praying for strength to ask Mona's forgiveness for the unkind things she had said about her. Every day she dreaded going to school, and her stomach knotted at the sight of Mona.

Finally on Friday, Jodi spotted her sitting alone on the school grounds during lunch break. She swallowed hard and approached her. Mona, her brown eyes flashing angrily, saw her coming and rose to walk away.

"Stop, Mona," Jodi said. "I want to talk to you." Mona hesitated, and then, brushing her hand through her short, dark hair, she sat back down on the bench. She held herself stiff and haughty.

Jodi swallowed again, and with her heart pounding, sat down on the bench. She opened her mouth, but the words would not come. It felt like her mouth was full of cotton.

"Well?" Mona said finally, shifting herself. "I don't have all day, you know!"

Jodi sent up a silent, urgent prayer for help. Then she began.

"I just want to say I'm sorry, Mona," she said. "I've been acting horrible to you. It's my temper, and I say things I don't really mean. I'm asking you to forgive me for spouting off the other day and saying those things about you." She paused and glanced down.

Mona sniffed. "Well, you *should* be sorry, I think!" she replied. "And don't come slobbering around me, begging for forgiveness! When you prove you're really sorry, I'll listen then!" She sniffed again and stomped off.

Jodi sat there, with her mouth open, watching her walk off. She felt cold, then hot with anger, and then confused. *What should I do now?* Someone sat beside her, and Jodi turned around. It was MaryAnn.

"What's the matter?" MaryAnn asked, gazing at her.

Jodi shook her head. "I just asked Mona to forgive me for calling her names the other day, and she wouldn't accept my apology! What do I do now?"

MaryAnn smiled. "I guess there's nothing you can do! Except pray for her, and show her by your actions that you really mean it. Don't you feel better for asking her forgiveness, anyway?"

Jodi leaned back and closed her eyes. Yes, it was a relief to have that over! The heaviness she had been carrying around all week was gone. And she felt the forgiveness of God as well.

She smiled. "I guess so. Thanks, MaryAnn."

When she got home there was a bulky letter waiting for

her. Brian peered over her shoulder as she picked it up.

"Oo-whee!" he shouted. "From Scot!"

She punched him and dashed up to her room, her cheeks burning. On her bed, she turned the envelope over and over. Why was it so bulky? Finally she opened it. Inside was a letter and a tiny package wrapped in fancy paper.

First she read the letter.

"Dear Jodi," he wrote, "I want to get this off, so you'll get it by your birthday." She paused and glanced at the calendar. Still over a month until her birthday! "Just something I picked up in Williams Lake, so you can remember me by. Everything is going fine here. The chapel was packed on Wednesday night, and Henry got up and gave his testimony in Chilcotin. His face just shines now!"

She smiled and blinked back the tears. "Evangeline's mother came back alone. She and Evangeline are going back up north. Evangeline is thrilled about that—she doesn't like it here. She has been asking some questions about the Bible, and we are writing to the missionary in their village. Reddy is really a good saddle horse now. I guess I have to admit that you're a pretty good horse trainer after all. Pretty, especially! I hope you are doing all right after your fall from the truck. Well, I can't think of anything else to say. Good-bye for now. Your friend, Scot. P.S. Mom says to say hi."

She read the letter over again and then laid it down on her bed. She picked up the tiny package. What could it be? With shaking fingers she unwrapped it and opened the box. She gasped with pleasure and surprise.

Inside lay a tiny golden heart on a delicate golden chain. In the center of the heart was her birthstone—an emerald.

Her mother knocked and came in just as she was lifting it out.

"Oh, Jodi!" Mrs. Fischer exclaimed, fastening it around her neck. "It's really lovely, and it looks so real! Now won't the other girls be jealous when you tell them where you got it!"

Jodi flashed her mother a smile and touched the locket, her blue eyes sparkling. "I hope not."